The wave of nausea hit Jessie suddenly.

"What's wrong?" Nick was at her side in an instant, putting his hand to her forehead. "You're sweating. I'll call a doctor. It could be something serious—your appendix. I know the symptoms."

"It's not that." Oh, Lord, she wasn't going to make it. Her stomach lurched again, and she ran to the bathroom.

"Jessica!"

She couldn't respond. Finally she stood and rinsed her mouth. She was brushing her teeth when Nick barged in. Her free hand went to her stomach. He stared at that hand.

"Baby?"

She nodded.

"Our baby?"

"Yes."

Nick grabbed for the door, but he didn't make it. Before Jessie's eyes, the sexiest, most confident man she knew dropped slowly to the floor in a dead faint.

Dear Reader,

I don't know about you, but my family and I can't pass by a fountain without throwing a coin in and making a wish.

Gina, Libby and Jessie are just like me. When they find themselves at the world-famous Trevi Fountain, they send out their wishes for happiness on those gilt-edged coins they toss. But sometimes, no matter what we *say* we want, our hearts know what we *truly* need....

So it is for Jessie here in Jo Leigh's *If Wishes Were...Daddies* and how it was for Gina in Debbi Rawlins's *If Wishes Were...Husbands* and for Libby in Karen Toller Whittenburg's *If Wishes Were...Weddings*.

I'm happy to say that some of my wishes have come true.... Let's see how it works out for Gina, Libby and Jessie in THREE COINS IN A FOUNTAIN. If you missed any of these stories, see the offer at the end of the book.

Happy reading!

Debra Matteucci
Senior Editor & Editorial Coordinator
Harlequin Books
300 East 42nd Street
New York, NY 10017

If Wishes Were...
DADDIES

JO LEIGH

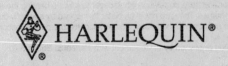

HARLEQUIN®

TORONTO • NEW YORK • LONDON
AMSTERDAM • PARIS • SYDNEY • HAMBURG
STOCKHOLM • ATHENS • TOKYO • MILAN • MADRID
PRAGUE • WARSAW • BUDAPEST • AUCKLAND

To Debi and Karen—what a team.
Grazie!

ISBN 0-373-16749-0

IF WISHES WERE...DADDIES

Prologue

As Jessica stepped out of the taxi in front of the villa, she debated finding a pay phone, calling her boss Jeff Hammond in Santa Monica and telling him just what he could do with all of his smart-ass remarks about how the only impulsive thing she'd ever done was call long distance before five.

If taking off during a work week, throwing some clothes together and flying to Rome wasn't impulsive, she didn't know what was. She hadn't even gone to her standing hair appointment. Of course, she'd been sure that nothing in the office would need her immediate attention and that Danny, her next-door neighbor, could water the plants. Impulsive didn't mean stupid. It meant free. Daring. Spontaneous. And what could be more spontaneous than whisking off to Italy to see a man she'd known only for a few months, just to surprise him for his birthday?

Nick. As she studied the front entrance to his

villa, she found herself smiling. He'd described his family home to her many times, in exquisite detail, but now she saw that he'd played down the majesty and beauty of the place. It was more a palace than a villa. She had a hard time believing Nick was able to pay for it on a commercial pilot's salary. No matter. It was a place of magic, and she didn't want to waste any more time on such practical trivia as mortgage payments.

The familiarity of the villa didn't do much to erase her overwhelming sense of unreality, though. Was she really here? In Rome, Italy? About to surprise a man she barely knew? Then she thought about the past three months.

Nick had come into her life like a tornado, hurling her old-fashioned but very safe notions of love and sex out the window, leaving her breathless. He'd shown her that she was a sensual woman every time she looked him in the eye. Now that she was in touch with that part of herself, she couldn't be content with her old life. Not with staid, predictable, workaholic Jessica. New vistas lay before her, and she wanted to explore each and every one.

She shifted her suitcase to her other hand and started up the steps. Halfway to the door, she stopped. Music, so soft she thought she might have imagined it, was coming from inside the villa. It wasn't just any music, either. It was "Un bel di" from *Madama Butterfly*. The aria that had been playing when she and Nick had kissed for the first time.

She retraced her steps to follow the music and went around to the east side of the villa. The side with the Romeo-and-Juliet balcony.

Nick had told her about the sturdy trellis, and how he had snuck out of his bedroom so many times, all in the pursuit of love.

As she rounded the corner, she saw it. It was exactly as she'd pictured it. The music was indeed coming from his bedroom, as if he'd anticipated her arrival. He probably had. Somehow he'd always known what she was thinking before she did. Wouldn't it be something to surprise him through that window? To appear as if by magic on the balcony?

The old Jessica wouldn't have dreamed or dared. The new Jessica tucked her suitcase behind a nearby shrub and prepared for her ascent. She couldn't climb all that way in her heels, but if she took them off, her hose would be ruined. The hell with it. Panty hose were dispensable in the quest for true romance.

She left her shoes by the suitcase, looked up, changed her mind and put her shoes back on. But the voice inside her head screamed ''Coward!'' and she slipped her shoes back off, and this time, she really did begin to climb.

It was scarier than she'd anticipated, but even

with her heart beating a mile a minute, she pressed on. The trick was not to look down.

Which, of course, she did the very next second. She stopped breathing, stopped everything, and clung tightly to the trellis, which was incredibly flimsy now that she thought about it. Okay, so maybe impulsive did mean stupid.

Gritting her teeth, she climbed, certain her demise was imminent. Wouldn't that be just perfect. Her one totally daring adventure, and she'd blow it by killing herself.

She took another step up, but her foot slipped, and if she hadn't been holding the trellis in a grip that melded her hand to the wood, she would have gone down. Instead, she just sort of kicked the air for a minute, all the while saying a prayer. Unfortunately, the only prayer that came to mind was "Now I lay me down to sleep." It worked, though, as her foot finally found the wooden bar.

She pressed herself tightly to the wall, wanting very much to cry uncle and scream. Nick would save her. That was romantic, too, wasn't it?

No. She must go on. It wasn't that far. Just a few more steps and she'd be at the balcony. Of course, once she got there, she had to figure out how to go from the trellis to the balcony.

Cursing the fact that she'd never been a Girl Scout, she ended up climbing higher. Then, in one of the most ungraceful maneuvers in recorded history, she flung herself over the edge of the balcony headfirst, so that she landed with the top part of her inside the balcony and the bottom part out. As she crawled forward, she had the sickening thought that Nick was watching her, laughing, pointing, changing his mind about loving her.

But when she was safe and she'd caught her breath and stood, she saw that she had been unobserved. The window was closed and the curtains drawn.

She straightened her hair a bit, adjusted her suit jacket and skirt, pushed the tall window open and climbed through. Now her heart was beating furiously again, but this time it was with sweet anticipation. In that flash of a moment, just before she saw him, she pictured his smile. That dreamy, sexy smile that had brought her several thousand miles from the safety of her home.

Only, he wasn't smiling.

Neither were the three other women in the bedroom with him.

Jessica opened her mouth, but no words came out. She looked from one woman to the next, noting somewhere in her brain that the three of them had the same shocked expression she must have on her face.

''Nick?'' the blonde to her right said.

''Nick?'' the brunette to her left said.

''Nick?'' Jessica said, mostly for the symmetry.

The object of their queries didn't even look embarrassed. He just mustered a sheepish grin and sat up straighter. "What a surprise," he said. "How nice of you all to drop in."

The woman in the nightgown, her long hair flowing almost to her waist, said something in Italian. Jessica didn't recognize the words, but the tone was unmistakable.

"Drop in?" the brunette to her right said. "Drop *in*? I came all the way from New York. Three planes. No sleep. And I turned down two courier jobs. I did *not* just drop in."

"Oh, Nick," said the blonde. She looked like the youngest of the three, barely in her twenties. "I told *everyone* we were going to get married!"

They all turned to look at Jessica, as if this were all a play, a tragedy, and it was her line. "So it's like this, is it?" she asked, amazed that she could think coherently, raise her eyebrow, cross her arms over her chest, when her dreams had just been squashed flat, her heart broken, her very soul shattered. "It was all a game?"

"It was never a game," Nick said.

"Right," Jessica said. "You meant everything you said?"

He hesitated for a long time, looking first at the Italian woman, then at the brunette, then at the blonde, then finally back at her. "Yes," he said.

She had to smile. He was taking an interesting

tack. No lies, no diversions. "So you love all of us?"

"Yes, Jessica. I love you all."

That almost did her in. She looked at the other women standing at her sides. She saw all her own emotions reflected in their eyes. Disbelief. Foolishness. Humiliation. Anger.

The Italian bombshell went on with her cursing, while the blonde met her gaze with a frown. "What should we do now?"

Jessica shook her head, feeling somehow worse for the younger woman than she did for herself. She turned to the brunette, so tall and striking and sure of herself. Only there was a questioning look in her eyes, too. "It is four to one," she said, giving Jessica a shrug. "We could take him."

Jessica sighed. She didn't want to beat him up. Well, she did, but she knew she wouldn't have the guts to do it. She'd used up her supply getting here. "I saw a small bistro just down the road," she said. "I imagine they serve liquor there. It is Rome, after all. I think I'm about to get well and truly drunk." She looked at her American companions. "If you'd care to join me?"

"Please stay, *carissima*," Nick said. "I can explain everything."

The taller woman looked back at Nick, still sitting in his bed. Jessica followed suit, impressed despite herself at his demeanor. He didn't look the least ruffled. A little chagrined, yes, but not mortally wounded. Not a chance. This must have been an old song for him. It was a brand-new melody for her, however. One she'd never sing again. Ever.

"Count me in," the brunette said. "I could use a shot or two."

"I'll go," the blonde said. "I've never been drunk before, but today seems like the perfect time to start."

"Yes," Jessica said. "It does, at that." She turned toward the door. No more balcony scenes for her. With as much dignity as she could muster in her stockinged feet, she walked away. Away from Nick and her fantasy, amazingly stupid in this new light, of romantic bliss. She should have known better than to listen to Puccini.

As she reached the door, she turned back one more time. "Happy birthday, you rat."

"To tar and feathers!"

Jessica lifted her wineglass and clinked it against Libby's. "Here, here."

"Ditto," Libby said, her enthusiastic nod making her blond hair fall lightly in her face. Then she clinked her glass against Gina's before she took another sip of wine. "Hot tar. Or, I know. We could rent a billboard at La Guardia and put a giant wanted poster up there."

"Yeah," Gina said. "You're really getting the

hang of this revenge scheme. I can't decide which one I like the best.'' The tall brunette had been quite clever in her plans to exact revenge upon the Italian gigolo. She'd not only come up with the excellent tar and feathers, but honey and ants, a short walk out of a 747 at thirty thousand feet— without a parachute—and Jessica's personal favorite, gelding the bastard.

"I can't believe I spent all that money to come here," Libby said. "I don't think I can afford a billboard."

Jessica had discovered that Libby was the youngest and least experienced of the three. The poor kid really had expected to marry Nick. But then, hadn't she? Maybe she'd never said it out loud, but hadn't she assumed that she and Nick would be together forever? "I spent a lot of money to get here, too," she said, sighing. "It just goes to show that you can't trust them. Not ever. Men are louses." That didn't sound right. "Lice?"

"Jessie, girl, you've got that straight," Gina said. "Men are from Mars, all righty," she said, signaling the waiter for more wine. "The question is, how do we get them to go back? Hey, a couple hundred torpedos would do the trick."

Jessica giggled. That alone told her she'd reached her desired goal of getting well and truly skunked. She should stop, sober up. Make arrangements to get back home. Oh, the hell with it. When the waiter came, she held out her glass. He filled it quickly, having wisely determined to leave the three crazy Americans alone.

"I think," Jessica said, leaning forward over the round wooden table, "that we should make a pact. Right here. Right now."

Both Libby and Gina also leaned in, each of them holding their wineglasses close for immediate access. Jessica looked around the small bistro to make sure no one was eavesdropping. It couldn't have been safer. Besides the waiter and the elderly woman behind the bar, there was only one other customer in the place, and his head was stuck in his newspaper. She did take a moment to appreciate the simple decor, the intimate feel of the place. It was quite romantic, and if Nick had turned out to be a man and not a louse, they might have had a lovely time here.

"Well?" Gina asked. "Let's hear about this pact."

Jessica turned back to her friends. They *were* friends. No, more like sisters. "I say we swear off men for good."

Both Gina and Libby nodded, but not very enthusiastically. Libby turned to Jessica. "For good? As in for the rest of our lives?"

Jessica nodded. "Yep."

"I don't know about that, Jessie girl," Gina said. "They can be pretty useful."

"As far as I can tell, there's only one thing a man can do that's of any damn use at all."

"But that one thing is a doozy," Gina said.

"What?" Libby asked, her brow furrowed. "What one thing?"

"There are ways to get around that," Jessica said. "You've heard of Bob? Our Battery-Operated-Boyfriend?"

"Oh!" Libby said, catching on.

"Jessie, hon. I don't think the answer is to cut yourself off from men entirely." Gina sipped her wine again, then put her glass down. "I think the trick is to know how to use them."

"Selectivity," Jessica said. "I can see your point."

"Right. Reel 'em in, throw back the little ones, put the big ones to work, then move on."

"Are you guys talking about what I think you're talking about?" Libby asked.

"Yeah," Jessica said. "Okay. Kind of like tissues. Take one, blow your nose, so to speak, then toss it."

"Sure," Gina said. "Why not? That way, there's no risk."

"Neat and tidy," Jessica added.

Libby frowned. "Are you saying that you never want to be in love? That you don't want to get married and have kids?"

Jessica stopped for a moment. Was that what she

was saying? She put her glass down. The tipsy feeling she'd had just seconds ago was gone now. She felt sober as a judge. "Libby, honey, I don't want to tell you not to keep trying. That's totally up to you, and whatever you decide to do is great. But for me? I don't like the odds."

Gina reached her hand over the table and wrapped it around Jessica's. "Maybe you can beat the odds. Maybe we all can."

Jessica squeezed her hand back. "Maybe. But I'm not betting the farm on it."

"You know what?" Libby said, her voice a little shaky but sincere.

Jessica looked at her and once again noticed how pretty she was. Blond, blue-eyed, baby-faced. Of course she shouldn't give up. There were probably a million guys who would love her in a minute. "What?"

"We're in Rome. And since we're here, I think we should go to the fountain."

"What fountain?" Gina asked.

"The Trevi Fountain. Like in that movie. *Three Coins in a Fountain*. You know, those three women were in Rome and they threw a coin in the fountain and made a wish? And Rossano Brazzi was in it, too."

Jessica had to smile. Such faith. Such innocence. To believe in wishes and old legends.

"There was that French guy, too," Gina said. "He was a count or something."

"Jessica," Libby said, turning to her. "Didn't you see it?"

Jessica nodded. "Sure I did."

"Then what do you say?" Libby didn't wait for an answer. She opened her purse and signaled the waiter. He came over and they got the money straightened out. Then he told them how to get to the famous fountain. It was actually very close.

Gina got up, and so did Libby. Jessica thought about turning them down, but when she saw their faces, so hopeful, just hours after being royally dumped, she couldn't say no.

She got up and followed Libby outside. The afternoon sun was bright and the streets were crowded with pedestrians, bicycles, Vespas and little tiny cars. It was so unlike Los Angeles. Jessica tried to see everything, from the street vendors to the little shops and the outdoor cafés, but Libby and Gina were walking very fast. In only a few moments, she got her first glimpse of the fountain.

There was a crowd standing around the magnificent landmark. She'd read all about it, of course. How it was one of the most beautiful and fanciful examples of Roman baroque. There was Oceanus on a seashell chariot drawn by two sea horses. There were the Tritons. And the statues flanking him, Abundance and Salubrity. On the plane over, she'd been impressed that the water flowing over the rocks to the oval pool had come from the Virgin Water spring, which Agrippa had brought to Rome for his baths in 19 B.C. Now she only had thoughts of drowning Nick.

"Excuse me, beautiful ladies."

Jessica looked around and saw a young boy of about twelve standing right behind them. "Are you speaking to us?"

"Beautiful lady, of course," he said. "You are the most pretty ladies here."

"Shouldn't you be in school?" Jessica asked.

The boy looked non-plussed. "Five thousand lire, and I tell you about the Trevi Fountain. The legend, the history. Only five thousand lire, beautiful lady."

Gina looked first to Libby, then to Jessica. She shrugged as Libby handed over a wad of paper money from her purse. "You'd better not run off," she said.

He took the money and stuffed it into his pocket quickly, but he didn't run. "I am Mario, a man of my word, lady," he said.

Jessica couldn't help but smile.

"This fountain is the most famous in all of Rome," he said, pointing like a weary tour guide. "There is a legend that, if one throws a coin into the fountain, then one must return to Italy and to Rome and this place. But I will tell you another legend...one that only some, such as myself, know for truth. This legend, it is very powerful magic. When the coin first touches the water of the Trevi, at that moment, if the heart makes a wish, it will come true. It cannot be otherwise. I tell you this because you are beautiful ladies and I wish for you that your special wish comes true.''

"Is that right?" Jessica said.

"I told you, lady. It's the truth. You throw your coin in now. You make a wish. It will come true."

Libby was the first one to get her coin out. "Come on," she said. "What do we have to lose?" She closed her eyes, and it wasn't hard for Jessica to imagine what her wish was. True love. Marriage. Kids. The whole works. Libby tossed her coin high in the air, and it fell in the fountain.

Gina already had her coin in her hand. It was a little harder to figure out her wish, but Jessica would have been surprised if it were all that different from Libby's. Gina's coin sailed through the air and landed near the statue.

"Your turn, Jessica," Libby said.

"I don't think so," she said.

"Come on," Gina prodded. "What's the worst that will happen?"

Jessica shook her head. It was all nonsense, wasn't it?

"Don't be a chicken," Gina said as Libby chimed in by clucking.

Jessica sighed and opened her purse. But she didn't look for her coin purse. Instead, she went to a little sewn pocket on the side, the same little pocket she sewed in every purse. The one that held her magic coin.

It wasn't really magic, but she'd called it that forever. Her grandmother had given it to her many years ago. It was phony silver and her name was etched on one side. Her grandmother had told her it would bring her luck. If ever she needed that luck, it was today.

She took the coin in her hand and closed her eyes. *"Please,"* she wished. *"Please don't let me be a fool for love. Not ever again. I just won't be able to stand it. And please, let me stop loving Nick."* She opened her eyes and threw the coin as high and as hard as she could. The silver trinket twirled in the air, caught the light, then fell into the water with no splash at all.

"I must also tell you the last part of the legend," the Italian boy said.

Surprised, Jessica turned to him, as did Libby and Gina.

"Only one wish will come true, beautiful ladies."

"What?" Libby said, her voice high. "Why?"

"What kind of scam are you running, you little twerp?" Gina demanded.

The boy shrugged. "I only tell the legend, lady. I don't make it up."

Libby looked at Gina, then at Jessica. She looked terribly forlorn, as if she'd just lost her last hope. While Jessica was fully aware of the absurdity of legends and coins and wishes, she understood how Libby felt. And although it wasn't nice, and it wasn't generous, she couldn't help making one last tiny wish.

Make it mine.

Chapter One

Nick Carlucci nodded as his sister went on with her tirade. He continued to listen, sort of, as Theresa listed all the reasons he was a selfish bastard, a discredit to the Carlucci name, a fool and a scoundrel. He meant her no disrespect, she certainly made some valid points, but his mind kept wandering back to the moment in his bedroom when Gina, Libby and Jessica had walked out the door. More specifically, he remembered seeing Jessica's feet. She hadn't been wearing shoes. Damned if she hadn't climbed his balcony.

What had it taken for her to do that? To come all the way to Rome to surprise him? To flout convention and pop into his bedroom unannounced, to face him without her shoes?

Of course, all three women had taken him by surprise. He felt terrible, even without Theresa's help. He owed them all an apology, which he would extend immediately. He doubted he could find them in the city, but he had their addresses in the States.

"You treat these women like playthings," Theresa shouted. "Like toys you can put back on the shelf when you're finished with them. You should be ashamed, Nicolo." She came over to his side of the large dining room table and put her hands on her hips. "I'm going to tell Mama."

Nick groaned. "Please, Theresa. I beg you…"

"No. This time you've gone too far. Did you see their faces? Did you hear the little one's voice? I'm telling Mama tonight."

Nick shook his head. "Can't you just shoot me? It would be better, believe me."

"Shooting would be too good for you. I ought to take you out and have you fixed."

Nick winced. "Is this how you treat your fiancé?"

Theresa straightened her back. "Tony would never do anything so…so…"

"Lousy?"

"Lousy!"

Nick stood up and took his sister's hand. "Theresa, darling, I never proposed to these women. I never lied to them. They assumed—"

She yanked her hand back. "They assumed that you loved them. That it was real." She sighed. "Big brother," she said, her voice suddenly soft, which was somehow much worse. "There are so many wonderful things about you. You're kind, you take care of us. You understand women better than anyone I've ever met, including Tony. But you hide your heart.'' She touched his cheek with her hand. ''You run like a boy from love. It's time to grow up, Nicolo. Time to be a man.''

Nick stepped back. ''Theresa, you're in love, so you think everyone should be in love.''

''No. It's not true. I care about you, and I want your happiness. You need to love one woman. And you need to let one woman love you back.''

''One woman is more than I can handle.'' He tried to smile. ''Ten, that's okay. But one?''

Theresa shook her head. ''I saw how you looked at her.''

''Who?''

''Don't play stupid. The one without the shoes.''

He looked at his cup of coffee on the table. ''Oh.''

''Go after her, Nick.''

''Then what?''

''Let it happen. Don't run away.''

''I can't do that.''

She shook her head sadly. ''I love you, Nick. But you're a coward. You try so hard not to be like Papa. But that was his life, not yours. It's time to let it go.''

''It's not that.''

''Liar.''

He couldn't look at her. Not when her words made his chest constrict so hard. "I have some apologies to make."

"Deliver hers in person, Nick. Don't run this time. If you do, you may never be able to stop running."

JESSICA POURED ANOTHER glass of sparkling water and lifted it in a silent toast to the beautiful city before her. She could see the fountain from her balcony, that gorgeous, well-lit, glimmering Trevi Fountain. So full of history and magic, so filled with wishes and dreams, it made her ache deep inside. Hers was a small wish, as wishes go. Nothing dramatic, no miracle needed. But oh, how she wanted it to come true.

She sipped her water, wondering if the unsettled feeling she had in her stomach was from heartache or the wine she'd had with Libby and Gina. She hadn't felt right all day. Wine had never affected her like this before, so it was undoubtedly love that was making her so queasy. Why was it that she was so smart about so many things, and so dumb about love? Genetics? Some past-life faux pas? Just plain bad luck? The answer didn't come, and the question, one she'd lived with for more years than she cared to think about, settled back down into its neat pocket, always available for examination whenever she let herself grow maudlin.

It wasn't right to be so melancholy in a city as gorgeous as Rome. But in her mind, Rome was Nick. Would always be Nick. And humiliation. Broken promises. Heartache. She grabbed the bottle and turned away from the view. It was better not to look.

She left the balcony and went to brush her teeth. Flipping on the bathroom light, she looked at herself in the mirror. Her nightgown was pathetic. It was something a child would wear, long, plain, white, not an ounce of cleavage visible. What made her think that a woman like her could attract a man like Nick? He had probably been with her for the novelty of it all. He'd probably never dated such a little prude before. Sighing, she picked up her toothbrush to begin the lonely ritual of getting ready for bed.

Once there, she tried hard to do the only thing that made sense. Cry herself to sleep. But, of course, it didn't work. Jessica didn't cry. She hadn't for years and years. She felt miserable, all right, but something seemed to be disconnected in her. Some emotional link. Her boss claimed it was something to do with the loss of control. Jessica didn't buy that. Well, not entirely.

It was true she wasn't the kind of person to let things get out of hand, but she didn't see what crying had to do with that. Jeff was always trying to come up with some heavy psychological reason for

Jessica's behavior. The man had taken one semester of abnormal psych. Hardly grounds for an educated opinion.

Be that as it may, Jessica certainly could have used some of Jeff's advice right now. How had she let herself get into this predicament?

Somewhere along the way, she'd taken a wrong turn. Was it when she'd first accepted Nick's invitation to dinner three months ago? Perhaps it was when she'd had that second glass of wine? No, it was after that. It was just a month ago, when they'd strolled down by the beach. When he'd taken her hand in his. When they'd made love.

That night was etched in her memory as clearly as the moonlight streaming through her window right now.... The soft, cool breeze. The feel of still-warm sand on her bare feet. The sound of the waves breaking on the shore. His voice when he'd asked her to come with him to Rome. The way he'd read her mind.

That was it, of course. The reason she couldn't just write him off and go on her merry way. Nick was a magician. He'd known immediately that she was scared, yet excited. Aching for adventure. That she'd been imagining—hoping—for his kiss for hours. More than that, he'd known she wasn't someone who cared easily. That she'd been hurt before and wasn't anxious to be hurt again.

Ironically, the one person who could really understand exactly how she felt, who would be able to offer her the kind of comfort she needed right now, was the man who'd made her feel this way. God, it was so confusing.

The only thing she knew for sure was that she couldn't stay in Rome one more day. Whatever it took, she was going home.

NICK STARED AT at the glittering coins that lay in the water. So many wishes from so many tourists, most of them gone unanswered and forgotten as the next bus and the bus after that came and went. Even now, so early in the morning, cameras clicked all around him, focusing on happy, tired sightseers anxious to toss their pennies into the Trevi, with hopes of coming back to Rome, or becoming rich beyond their dreams, or, more likely, of finding true love.

Nick could have told them that the coins they tossed were swept out each week and sent to the city coffers to be distributed to charitable organizations. That there was no magic in the water at all. But he wouldn't tell, even if someone asked. Everyone needed dreams. Even cynical Italians.

He hadn't known that until yesterday. Until Jessica Needham had walked out of his life.

He cringed. He'd made plenty of mistakes before, but nothing to compare with the mess he'd made with those three women. Libby and Gina were both wonderful, unique beauties, and he felt like hell that he'd angered and disappointed them. He'd never meant to hurt them. Or to make anyone believe he wanted marriage. But, as Theresa had pointed out so loudly, he hadn't done anything to dissuade them, either.

He'd spent the evening writing all three of them letters. Apologies. This morning, he'd gone to the post to send them off, but he'd only sent two. He had the one to Jessica in his pocket right now.

Her letter had taken the longest. Most of the night. He'd thrown away draft after draft, unable to find the right words. He'd never found them. How could he tell her how he felt about her when he didn't know himself? With Libby and Gina, he was clear. He was sorry he'd led them to believe there was more to him than the selfish bastard he was. Sorry they'd pinned any hopes or dreams on him. Sorry they'd come all the way to Rome. He'd sent them both the cost of their tickets, even though he knew that the gesture wouldn't help much. He had to confess, it did ease his guilty conscience a bit. But with Jessica, his apologies fell flat.

He wanted to explain that his invitation to come to Italy had been sincere. That, if it hadn't been for the odd twist of fate that had brought the three women to his bedroom at the same moment, he would have been overjoyed to see her.

What he didn't understand was, why? Why

couldn't he find the right words for Jessica? Why was losing her unacceptable? He didn't love her. He barely knew her. Of course he'd enjoyed making love with her, but that wasn't reason enough for this preoccupation. Something strange was going on. It troubled him enough to bring him out to the fountain. Right to the edge, where he could stare at the coins. To wonder if she'd come here. If she'd made a wish—and if that wish had anything to do with him.

He felt in his pocket, but instead of bringing out her letter, he brought out a coin of his own. Even as he contemplated the act, he knew it was foolish. Who believed in this nonsense anymore? Yet there he was, holding the coin just so, moving his arm down, then up. Watching as it spun in the air, then arced gracefully toward the water. Noting the small splash and the slow descent to the bottom. Staring at silver coins, currency from all over the world. Wishes from strangers. Hopes and dreams. Nonsense. Superstition.

He shook his head, knowing better. Knowing what he wished for had no chance of coming true. Knowing he was going to go after her all the same.

JESSICA FELT LIKE HELL. She'd been sick this morning, really sick, and had called down to the concierge for the name of an English-speaking doctor. Gina, who'd surprised her by showing up late last night asking for a place to crash, had tried to get her to eat some toast and tea while she'd waited out the hour before her appointment, but that hadn't worked. She'd said goodbye to Gina, telling her she felt better and promising to keep in touch. Now her stomach was upset, her head ached, and all she wanted was to be back home. The flu was bad enough, but the flu in a foreign country? She moaned, pressing the flat of her hand against her tummy.

Sitting on the cold examination table, clutching the ridiculous paper gown around her, she thought she'd never been quite this miserable in her entire life. Even if she could get a flight, how could she fly home today when she felt like this? Besides, it wouldn't be right to spread her germs to a plane full of unsuspecting travelers.

Why had she ever come to Rome in the first place? Visions of Nick hadn't left her for a moment. Even when she'd been at her worst, the memory of her moment in his villa swam vividly in her head. At least the humiliation was becoming familiar. Sort of comforting, in a way. It wasn't the first time she'd made a fool of herself, just the most impressive.

Her stomach lurched again, and she prayed for death. Quick, peaceful and final. Instead, the doctor walked in. He was an older man, his silver hair styled to within an inch of its life, his suit expensive underneath his lab coat. She sighed and tried for a smile. It didn't work.

"Now, let's see what we have here," the doctor said, flipping open her chart.

Jessica closed her eyes, hoping the man had some magic pills in his bag. No one could feel this awful forever. Right?

LOS ANGELES INTERNATIONAL Airport. The most wonderful sight in the world as far as Jessica was concerned. She was home. She'd never wanted to be anywhere so much in her life. It had cost her, but she'd managed to change her flight plans yesterday afternoon. She wouldn't have cared if it had meant spending her last dime. She needed to leave Rome. She needed to be home. She needed help.

It still hadn't hit her fully. Not really. Not all the implications. All she knew was that she didn't have the flu. She wasn't lovesick. She wasn't even dying.

She was pregnant. With Nick Carlucci's child.

Chapter Two

It took him three days to get to America. Another to catch a flight from New York to Los Angeles. He'd had to do some fancy footwork to make the flights, and to take time off, but in the end, he'd gotten here. By the time he'd checked into his hotel room, he was exhausted, hungry, irritable, and completely convinced he was insane.

What was he doing here? Six thousand miles to say he was sorry? To a woman whom he barely knew, and would never see again? It was crazy. Almost as crazy as climbing up a balcony barefoot.

He smiled as he unpacked. Maybe that was it. The whole reason he'd changed his flight schedules, canceled plans, chased her halfway around the world. She'd done something so brave that he couldn't chicken out himself, could he?

All he was going to do was apologize. Explain about Gina and Libby. Tell her he wished he could have shown her his city. Then he would leave. He could return home then and face Theresa and Mama. And one thing was for sure—no more American women.

He'd fallen in love with America the first time he'd set foot here, all those years ago. His decision to go to university in Los Angeles had been the best one of his life. The women he'd met! They'd all been so different, so American. They'd laughed so hard, loved so freely. He'd never wanted to go. He'd thought for a while that he wouldn't. That he'd stay in this country. But the family needed him. So he'd done the next best thing. He'd taken the job with Alitalia, with runs to and from the States.

But America, especially California, always beckoned. He felt as much at home here as he did in Rome. More, maybe. There was something about the sunshine, the ocean... Who was he kidding? It was the women that kept him coming back here. *Jessica.*

How to explain Jessica? What made him pursue her, even when he realized he didn't know her at all? There was something inside her that called to him. Like a diamond waiting to be polished. A flower about to bloom. Jessica was on the brink of discovery, and he wanted to be there when it happened.

She was so closed, so proper. Yet underneath... There was a fire inside her. He'd felt it immediately. A heat so hot it would melt them both. Making love to Jessie once again would be—

Impossible.

He unzipped his suitcase and hung up his clothes, angry at himself for thinking such foolish thoughts. He was here to apologize. That's all. To assuage a guilty conscience. To get his mother off his back.

No more American women. Good Italian girls for him, from now on. He understood Italian girls. They understood him. *Basta.* Enough. No more crazy thoughts.

He finished his unpacking, then called down to room service. A quick meal, a nap, a shower, then he would go. It would be close to five o'clock then. She'd be ready to leave her office. He'd catch her there, ask her to dinner. They'd have one final meal. Then he'd bow out.

JESSICA HUNG UP the telephone and looked over at her boss. Jeff Hammond sat on the couch in her office, drawing furiously on his sketch pad as if he were angry at the world. Of course, Jessica knew it wasn't anger that made his fingers fly, but concern. For her. Ever since she'd come to work yesterday and told Jeff about what had happened with Nick, her best friend had been in a tizzy. Then again, that's what Jeff did best.

"It's going to be all right," Jessica said, as she

got up to fix herself another cup of tea. "I just need a little time to think things through."

His pencil quieted. When Jessica turned from the teapot, Jeff was staring at her. They were so different. Jeff was the height of artistic élan, and looked the part. Terribly tall and handsome, he wrapped his clients around his little finger, and intuitively knew what decor would work and what wouldn't. He was the right-brain side of Main Street Designs, while Jessica, with her tailored suits and, as Jeff put it, her anal-retentive obsessiveness, was the left-brain side. Together, they made one terrific person. Apart, they needed each other for balance, and more important, for friendship.

Jessica finished pouring the hot water, then took her cup over to the couch. She sat next to him, once again incredibly grateful to have someone to confide in. Well, sort of. She'd told Jeff what had happened in Rome, but she hadn't sprung the news about the baby yet. She needed some more time for that one. Time to adjust to the fact that it was even real.

"All I'm saying is that you wasted a perfectly good trip to Italy all because of one jerk. You should have stayed," Jeff said.

"I couldn't. Not after walking in on Nick with three other women."

"You let him off too easy. That Gina, she had the right idea. Gelding."

"She was something. I liked Libby, too. At least the guy had some taste."

"What gets me is that I liked him. I really did. I thought you two had a damn good chance of making it work."

"So I wasn't the only one blinded by his looks?"

Jeff shook his head. "Sweetie, you know I love you, but if I thought I'd have a chance with him I'd have mowed you over like yesterday's grass."

Jessica laughed. "I wouldn't wish him on you. You deserve better."

"And so do you." He looked at her critically, his brows furrowing as he studied her face. "This has really thrown you, hasn't it? You don't look good."

"Thanks."

"I mean it. Your complexion is all off. Maybe you ought to get a massage. Or a colonic."

"What a choice."

"Well, you need something."

"Ever hear of jet lag?"

"Hmm. I don't know."

Jessica drank some tea and sighed as the warmth spread to her stomach. Her very unreliable stomach. Just her luck that this little surprise pregnancy had also brought her a raging case of morning sickness. A case that, unfortunately, didn't know how to tell time. She felt queasy all day, every day. "I just wish I could forget about him," she said, purposely changing the subject. "I just can't seem to shake him."

"Nick?" Jeff asked.

"No, Tom Cruise. Of course, Nick."

"Time will take care of that," Jeff said. "Although it took me a hell of a long time to get over Craig. But then, we'd been together for two years."

"And I barely know Nick."

"Maybe it was a misunderstanding. Maybe he really does care for you."

"Please, Jeff. Don't make me laugh."

"Okay, so it was a long shot. It just bothers me to see you so miserable."

"I'll get over it."

"I know."

"I just wish I wasn't so stupid about men. I seem to have an uncommon knack for picking out louses."

"Come on, Jess. That's not true."

"No? When's the last time I had a healthy relationship?"

Jeff sipped some coffee. "What about Charlie?"

"The one who stole my underwear?"

"Oh, yeah. I forgot about that."

"He did look pretty good in them. I'll give him that."

Jeff smiled. "Wow, I hadn't thought of that in a long time. That was some Christmas."

"I'll say."

"What about Trevor? He was nice."

"Trevor was a boob. The man could only talk about one thing—his blessed computer."

"Yeah. Okay. I admit it, your luck hasn't been all that great when it comes to men." Jeff sighed. "For what it's worth, this time I thought you'd found someone special."

"So did half the women in America, evidently."

"He just sat there? Smiling?"

"Oh, I think he was uncomfortable. But man, he was smooth. He acted like four women showing up in his bedroom happened twice a week. I mean, he hardly blinked."

"The bastard."

"It was my own fault. It was crazy of me to go in the first place."

"It wasn't crazy. It was brave and wonderful. I'm still so proud of you I can't stand it."

Jessica laughed. "Brave? Wonderful? I just spent four thousand dollars to find out I'm a chump. A world-class chump."

Jeff leaned forward and took Jessica's hand. "No. You're not the chump here, kiddo. You did great. You followed your heart, and no matter what the outcome, doing that was absolutely the right thing to do. Remember that. And don't let one Italian idiot take any of that away from you. I'm proud of you, sweetie. Prouder than I can say."

Jessica's chest tightened. For a woman who

didn't cry, she'd been awfully close in the last few days. "Thanks. But I think next time I make a fool out of myself, I'll try to do it on American soil."

"Oh, please. He did everything but whisk you away on a magic carpet. You wouldn't have been human if you hadn't fallen for him."

"It just scares me. I mean, you know me. I'm a judicious person. A thinking person. And I not only slept with this man, whom I barely knew, I flew to Italy on a whim." She looked down at her teacup. "But that's not the worst of it."

"Go on."

Jessica slowly looked up. "I still care about him, Jeff. Way, way too much."

"Hey, it's only been a few days. What did you expect?"

"I didn't expect this." She stood up, suddenly anxious to move. "I didn't expect that I'd care. I don't know him. He made no promises. It's just not possible that I actually fell—" She stopped dead still.

"Fell in love?" Jeff said, his voice low and kind.

Jessica didn't turn to look at him. She just nodded, shame and humiliation flooding through her veins. "How stupid is that?"

"It's not stupid at all. It's human. And even you can't deny that beneath those prim little suits, you're only flesh and blood."

"But it hurts."

"I know, honey. It's not easy being part of the great unwashed, but there you have it. Love hurts. It sucks. It's not pretty. Except..."

"Except when the guy loves you back."

"Uh-huh."

"So why didn't he?" Jessica whispered. She slowly turned, now that she'd asked the question aloud. The question she'd been asking herself for three days. "Why didn't he love me back?"

"Oh, Jess. Who knows? There could be a million reasons."

"I know. Really. What did I expect?" She waved her hand, as if swatting away her own silliness. "Besides, I didn't love him. Not the real kind of love. I couldn't have. We weren't together long enough for that to happen, right? I'm just being a sentimental fool."

"I wouldn't be so quick to dismiss your feelings. I think you did feel something very special for Nick. I'd never seen you like that before."

"Like what?"

"So happy."

Jessica smiled. "Yeah, I was floating there for a while, wasn't I?"

Jeff nodded. "It was great. It can be like that again, you know."

"No, I don't think so."

"Nick isn't the last man out there."

"He's the last man for me. I'm not going to go

through this again, Jeff. Not for anything. I may be dumb, but I'm not stupid.''

Jeff stood up. ''You don't have to decide everything right now. What you do have to do is make sure you're taking care of yourself. So don't rule out that colonic. It can do wonders for jet lag.''

''Thanks,'' she said, looking up at him. ''I'll think about it.''

''Do that. And stop beating yourself up. You didn't do anything wrong.''

Jessica smiled. But all she could think of was if she didn't do anything wrong, why was she being punished?

NICK LIKED HIS HOTEL ROOM. It was midway between Jessica's office and apartment, it was large and bright and very American. The first thing the bellboy had shown him was the cable television.

He'd already eaten, napped and cleaned up, and now he sat on his balcony considering his options. He wanted everything to go well. Of course, she could just throw him out on his ear, but he had a feeling she wouldn't. Not at her office. Not in front of Jeff and her colleagues. She'd act civilized, which would give him the foot in the door he needed.

But would she go out with him again? Would she give him a chance to explain? Somehow, he had to get her alone. Away from the office. He needed to get back to the way it had been before Rome.

He'd thought about that all the way across the ocean. He hadn't slept. He never did when he flew. But this time, he hadn't read or watched the movies. At least not the movies they were showing on the screen. He just relived the movie in his mind. Each moment spent in the company of Jessica played over and over in his head.

She had such a wonderful laugh, although she didn't use it often enough. He remembered a night at the beach, at Malibu. Her hand nestled in his, her shoulder just touching his own. She'd taken off her shoes, and they'd walked the shore, marveling at the moon and the white glitter the waves left in their wake. He'd made her laugh that night with stories that had once been so familiar, then transformed by the listener. He'd laughed, too. But mostly out of pure pleasure at the woman beside him.

He wanted to hear that laugh again. To make things right with her. Then what? What was he going to do if he got his wish? If Jessica forgave him?

That was problem number two. According to his sister, he had only one option—marry her. But Theresa was Theresa, and marriage was on her mind a lot these days. He didn't have much faith in the institution, himself. Theresa dismissed his opinions as his attempt to stay a child, to run from commitment. But that wasn't it. He just didn't understand why so many people wanted to marry.

Marriage had made sense at one time. Back when people lived to a ripe old age of thirty, if they were lucky. A lifetime commitment then meant ten, fifteen years. A marriage now could last fifty, sixty years! It was unnatural. Terrifying. No sane person could want that. And Jessica was the sanest person he knew.

They hadn't discussed the subject, but he did remember that she'd told a joke about the terrible divorce statistics once. That had to mean something.

Now, if she would only understand what had taken place at the villa...

He grabbed his sunglasses and went downstairs. The valet brought him his rented Porsche. Surprisingly, he found himself a little nervous. Not in the usual way. He always looked forward to a conquest, but now his stomach was a little tight, his breathing a little rapid. Maybe it was because this time he had a bigger wall to climb over. Jessica was formidable. That was undeniable. Then again, that would make it all the sweeter when she succumbed. And if she didn't? That wasn't something he cared to think about.

He pulled out of the drive and headed toward her office. The first thing he saw was a car completely covered in grass. Real grass! He laughed. America.

THERE WAS NO REASON for Jessica to stay at the office. All her phone calls had been returned. Everyone, including the secretaries, had gone home already. She'd paid the bills, done a backup of her computer files. She'd even repotted her little violet. But home wasn't a place she wanted to go. Not yet, at least. She wished Jeff was here. No, that's actually not what she wished. But what she wished for, she couldn't have.

Damn it, why couldn't she stop thinking about Nick? He had been a mistake. If the world were fair, she would have been depressed for a few weeks, eaten way too much chocolate and moved on with her life. But no. The world wasn't the least bit fair. She was going to have to live with this mistake for the rest of her life.

Her hand went to her belly. Not that she would ever think of this little one as a mistake. Girl or boy, she'd love it with all her heart. As for adoption? Nope. There was no way she would ever give up her child. Nick's child.

Would this baby always remind her of the love she almost had? Of the magic that had been in her life for a heartbeat, then vanished like dust in the wind? Or would time sculpt new memories? She wanted to remember some things. The night on the beach. That first dinner. The night they'd made love and she'd let go for the first time in her whole life.

All she wanted was to forget one summer day in

Rome. One climb up a balcony. That couldn't be too hard, could it? Unfortunately, only time would tell. Right now, she had some decisions to make. She had to tell Nick about the baby. But that could wait a bit. At least until she had time to adjust to the pregnancy herself. Nick came from strong roots. He was an only son. The family wouldn't ignore an heir.

It would be simpler for her not to tell Nick. To keep the baby a secret and just raise him alone. But would that be fair to the child? To grow up without a father? To deny him his heritage?

Lord, she was confused. And her stomach was acting up again. Great. Jessica opened her bottom drawer and pulled out her bag of crackers. She'd heard that dry crackers were supposed to help, but she wasn't so sure. Of course, she wasn't sure about anything. She barely knew the first thing about being pregnant. That's what she'd do. Go home and finish reading her pregnancy books. So far, they'd been illuminating.

Having a child was no different from starting a business, after all. She'd done a great deal of preparation before she'd undertaken that task, and she'd do the same for the baby. Once she had it figured out, then she'd deal with telling Nick.

One step at a time. That was her motto. Take it slow, don't be rash. The only real mistakes she'd made in her life had all come out of impulsive decisions. Going out with Nick. Making love to Nick. Going to Rome to see Nick.

The front door buzzed and she got up quickly, wondering who could be here this late in the day. Federal Express usually came by earlier, and besides, she hadn't called them. Perhaps a client?

She brushed some errant crumbs off her blouse and hurried to the reception area. When she turned the corner, her welcoming smile froze on her lips.

"Hello, *cara*."

"Nick." She couldn't believe it. It must be some kind of trick. "What...?"

"I've come to talk to you, Jessica."

She shook her head slowly. Then things started going badly. Really badly. She covered her mouth with her hands and dashed off to the rest room.

Nick blinked at Jessica's sudden disappearance. He winced when he heard her in the rest room. Then he sighed. Perfect. "That went well," he said, to no one in particular. "Better than I'd hoped for."

Chapter Three

Jessica sat down on the chair in the rest room and tried to pull herself together. Her stomach had stopped rebelling, and she'd washed her face and brushed her teeth. She'd even pulled a brush through her hair. Now she had to go back out there and face him. Unless, of course, she just stayed in the bathroom for the rest of her life. Which, as each minute dragged on, was looking better and better.

What was he doing here? Did he honestly think she wanted to be a part of his worldwide harem? Maybe Italian women didn't mind the whole group thing, but she wasn't Italian.

Oh, God. She'd thrown up. So much for having some time to think about how to tell Nick she was pregnant. Dammit. She really wasn't ready to deal with this. Not yet. She needed more time!

"Jessica?"

She froze. He was right outside the bathroom. Oh, Lord. No, no, not yet.

"Are you all right, *cara?*"

"Yes," she said, but it came out in sort of a squeak. She cleared her throat and tried again. "Yes, I'm fine. Just a moment."

"Can I bring you some water? An aspirin?"

"No, no. Just have a seat. I'll be right out." She waited to see if he'd press her, but he didn't. Why couldn't Jeff have been here? Or one of the other guys? Why hadn't she gone home?

Jessica stood up and checked her makeup in the mirror. Her eyes frightened her—she looked absolutely panicked. Like a deer caught in headlights. No, more like a raccoon, with her mascara all smeared. She grabbed a tissue and started wiping the mess, willing herself to calm down.

Okay, the thing to do was to be rational. So she didn't have time to make her lists of opening lines. She could improvise. A, she didn't have to tell him about the pregnancy right this minute. If he asked her about feeling ill, she'd change the subject. B, she didn't have to talk to him for a long time. She could say she had an appointment. C, she had every reason to boot him out of here without so much as a word. He was the one with the all-girl band in his bedroom, not her. D, she wasn't going to die. People didn't die from situations like this.

Her eye makeup looked halfway decent, although if she'd had the time, she would have reapplied it all. She'd have added some blush, too. She looked pale as a ghost. No lipstick, either. Oh, well, what difference did it make? She wasn't trying to impress anyone. Especially not Nick.

Her breathing had calmed, too. Good. Okay. She had her bearings again. She could do this. She really could.

Straightening her back, she turned to the door and opened it. Her heart thudded so hard in her chest she thought it might just pop right out, but she did it. She walked out. He stood up to face her, concern all over that beautiful Italian mug of his.

"Are you all right?" he said again.

She nodded. "What are you doing here, Nick?"

He moved toward her. She wanted to tell him to stop. The nearer he got to her, the clearer her face would become. And she didn't trust her face right now. Normally, she had no problem masking her emotions. But not today. Not with him.

"I came to talk to you. I didn't know you were feeling ill. I'm concerned. Perhaps we should go to the doctor? I have a car, I can drive you."

"No need. I'm feeling fine now. What did you come to talk to me about?"

He stood just a few feet away from her, and that wasn't fair at all. Not because he was getting a good look her way, but because she could see too much of him. His face killed her. It was just so perfect. She remembered looking into those eyes and believing what she saw there. Believing that he felt something. That the look of love, of tenderness, of need, was something unique, meant only for her. Ha. It was probably patented. He probably looked adoringly at his butcher when he got a nice hunk of sirloin.

"I didn't want you to misunderstand what you saw in Rome."

"That's not the part I misunderstood. I was confused about the part here in Santa Monica. The part in Rome was crystal clear."

"No, no. You see, that's why I'm here. To explain."

"You don't need to. You don't owe me anything. I goofed up. I thought we had something, and we didn't. Don't worry, I don't blame you. It was my own fault. I never should have gone. And I certainly never should have barged into your bedroom like that."

"I don't want you to blame yourself. What you did was wonderful. Jessica, you climbed the balcony. I barely believed it, but you did. That was *magnifico, cara.* I only wish fate hadn't played such a trick on us."

"Nick, fate did me a favor. An expensive favor, but that's the way it goes. I thought you were someone else. That's all. No harm, no foul. So thanks for stopping by, but it's late, and I need to go."

He took another step toward her. She almost backed away, but she didn't. She had to stand her ground now, or forever regret it. It wasn't easy. He was too close. Something happened to her when he got this near. Her chest constricted, her knees got weak, and her resolve just sort of slipped away. He'd done that to her from the beginning. From that first moment.

"Please. Don't let it end like this. Have dinner with me, Jessica. One dinner." He smiled. "You know, between us, we flew around the world to see each other. That has to mean something. It would hurt me very much to leave now, without talking."

She felt herself weaken. Like ice cracking chip by chip, her resolve faltered, then gave way. She nodded. It was only for one dinner. And he had traveled an awfully long way.

"Would you like to go home first? I can come pick you up later. Or we could go now. Whatever you want."

"Yes, I'd like to go home first," she said. "Wait, no. We might as well go now."

He grinned as he closed the last bit of distance between them and put his palm on the small of her back. She jumped, unprepared for the touch, completely unprepared for the jolt that went through her. "No, I'll go home," she said, her voice as wobbly as her legs.

He looked at her, clearly confused. "You don't feel well, do you? I'll take you home. Make you some minestrone."

She laughed, a short burst that surprised her as much as it did him. But the image of him making her the Italian equivalent of chicken soup struck her as absurd.

"You don't think I know how to cook?"

"I can't picture, it, no."

He put his hand up to his heart, as if she'd wounded him mortally. For some reason, she found herself focused on his incredible shirt. Blue silk. Tailored exquisitely. The detail on the cuffs alone was a work of art.

"I'm wounded," he said. "All proper Italian men cook. I can make a pasta that would change your religion."

The idea of pasta, of thick tomato sauce, made her stomach lurch again, and for a horrible moment, she thought she was going to give him a repeat-and-up-close reenactment of her welcome. She stood still, willing it away, and, gratefully, it worked. But dinner wasn't going to happen. Not tonight.

"Actually," she said, "I think I will go home. But alone. I'm not feeling well, you're right. I think I just need to put myself to bed."

He scowled at her. "You don't look so good. I'll take you."

"I have my car here. I'm perfectly fine to drive—"

"No. You can get your car tomorrow. Now, you come with me."

"Nick, I'm fine. I—"

He went to her desk and picked up her purse. "Is this all you need?"

"Yes, but—"

"Come, we go." He came back to her, put his arm around her waist and walked her toward the door.

She sighed. She didn't have it in her to argue. Not when it felt so comforting to have him to lean on. A small part of her was completely appalled that she was letting him take charge like this, after what he'd done, but the much bigger part felt weepy and needy and, frankly, too tired to be self-righteous.

She let him take her outside, but stopped him to fish her keys out of her purse and lock the door. For a quick second, she was lost in a sense of déjà vu. She'd locked this door a month ago, with Nick waiting by her side. But last time, she'd been almost giddy with expectations, and this time she was nauseous because she was expecting. A lot can change in a month.

Nick put his arm back around her waist and walked with her toward the parking lot. Being this close to him was nerve-racking, and she wanted to pull away. But she didn't. If she pulled away, he'd know she was bothered by his nearness. He didn't deserve to know that.

Of course, he had a Porsche. She tried to imagine him in a station wagon, with a baby seat in the back. It didn't gel. If anyone had ever fit the description of jet-setter, it was Nick Carlucci.

He held the door open for her and she climbed in, wondering what the heck she was going to talk about on the drive home. And how quickly she could ask him to leave once she got there. It wasn't as if she owed him anything. But...

She tried to think how Jeff would handle the situation. Of all her friends, he was the one who knew how to deal with messy relationships. Jeff was the one person she knew who could actually think of his fantastic rejoinders when he needed them. Not three hours later, like her. She'd actually written down several of his more memorable lines, but for the life of her, she couldn't think of one right now.

Nick got in beside her and buckled up. She followed suit and stared straight ahead as he turned the key. Once they got on the road, she dared a glance at him. His hands gripped the steering wheel so tightly they were white. He, too, was looking straight ahead, and his jaw muscle flexed with tension.

That made her feel better. Somehow, she hadn't expected Nick to be nervous. It was still a little unbelievable. She never thought of him as anything but suave and cool and sophisticated. Even during that dreadful soap opera moment in his bedroom, he'd been the picture of debonair. And now he was nervous? With her?

"You said you wanted to explain," she said as they waited for the light to change on Wilshire. "Now seems as good a time as any."

"Here? Now?"

Was that a hint of panic she heard? That shouldn't make her happy, but it did. She'd never seriously considered the option of torturing Nick. But hey, she was flexible. "Yes. Right now. Or never."

"But, dinner. You said..."

"Nick, it's now or never."

The panic that had been in his voice had traveled to his eyes. She'd never seen this side of him before. It was most interesting.

"Very well, but you're not being fair."

"Well, there isn't a whole lot that's fair in this world, so you should be used to it. Now, quit trying to change the subject and explain."

He said something to himself, which she didn't quite catch. It was undoubtedly Italian, and definitely one of the words not covered in her Italian-English dictionary. "All right," he said, "I'll explain."

She waited. And waited. Finally, he said, "First,

I want you to know that I meant it when I asked you to come back with me to Rome.''

He looked at her briefly, then at the road. ''I wanted to show you my home. My city. I'm sorry you left so quickly. I would still like to show you my Rome, *cara*.''

''Go on.''

''I didn't invite Gina or Libby. In some twist of fate, they both decided to come visit on a whim.''

''Some whim.''

He frowned. ''That's the right word, isn't it?''

''Oh, yes. It's right next to folly in the thesaurus.''

''Bad timing, yes. Folly? No.''

''And what about your Italian friend?''

Nick shook his head. ''She was no friend, Jessica. She's my sister. Theresa.''

''Oh?''

''Yes.''

''In her nightgown?''

''She's living in the villa with me until she gets married. She came up to ask me about lunch.''

''I don't know. She seemed awfully upset to be your sister.''

''You don't know Theresa. She is often upset. More lately, it seems.''

''Any particular reason?''

''She believes it's time for me to settle down.''

Jessica's stomach constricted. She gripped the

door handle, not daring to look at him. What would Theresa say when she found out Nick was going to be a father? She took a deep breath. "And how do you feel about that?"

Nick didn't answer right away. He turned onto her street and drove all the way to her apartment building. He waited until she handed him her card key, then he drove them down into her parking garage. Before he gave her back the key, he turned off the motor. Then he looked at her. It was dark, but she could see him clearly enough. The panic was gone from his eyes. But she couldn't read him.

"I'm not sure, Jessica. A part of me thinks she's right. It is time for me to settle down. But how do I settle down when one week I'm in Rome, the next in New York? Or Paris? Or Brazil?"

Her breath left her slowly and her grip eased. She felt a little foolish for hoping. She wasn't even sure what she was hoping for. That he wanted to settle down with her? He barely knew her. That he wanted to have children? That he loved her? That was the most ridiculous hope of all. "Of course," she said. "Why settle down when the whole world is your playground?" She smiled. "It must all be like a giant buffet to you. A little Italian appetizer here, a little French there. Some American morsels to cleanse the palate."

Nick opened his mouth, then shut it. He looked at his lap for a moment, then swung his gaze back to meet hers. "Yes," he said, his voice soft, and almost shy. "It has been. But lately…"

"Yes?"

"Lately it hasn't been so appealing."

"Why not?"

He shrugged. "I don't know. But I think…I've thought about you a great deal, Jessica."

"Really?"

He nodded. "I wrote you many letters. Then threw them all away. I couldn't find the words to explain."

"What, Nick? It seems pretty simple to me. You asked me to come to Rome but didn't expect me to actually show up. You asked Gina and Libby, and didn't expect them to show up, either. But we did. And now you want us all to forget that and go on as if nothing happened. To not care that we're just notches on your very large belt?"

"I didn't invite anyone but you."

"That doesn't change anything."

"Of course it does."

"What? I'm supposed to be pleased that my notch is bigger? It doesn't change the quantity, Nick."

He leaned forward, but she held up her hand. "Look, I'm not here to sit in judgment of how you lead your life. That's completely up to you. All I can do is make choices. And I choose not to be one of your ports in a storm. I'm not good at sharing. I never have been.''

''I see,'' he said. ''So my choice is you alone, or nothing?''

''That's right. And I think we both know what your choice will be.'' She undid her seat belt and opened her door. ''Thanks for the ride home, Nick. Take care.'' She shut the door, the sound loud and final in the small garage. She was tired, more tired than she could ever remember being in her whole life. It was an effort to move one foot after the other. She waited to hear the car engine come to life, but it didn't. She got to the elevator and pushed the button, then turned.

Nick was standing by the car. He shut his door and walked toward her.

She should tell him to stop, to leave now, and be done with it. Of course, she'd have to contact him about the baby, but she'd rather wait to do that until he was a half a world away. Until she had time to think clearly, rationally, and not care so damn much that he found it so easy to tell her goodbye.

He approached her slowly, as if with each step he might turn on his heel. She willed the elevator doors to open, but they didn't. Nick reached her first.

''I would like to come upstairs,'' he said. ''Please.''

''I don't think that's a very good idea.''

"I don't mean you any harm."

"Of course you don't. But you'll end up hurting me all the same."

"It was never my intention. I care for you, Jessica."

"And I care for you, Nick. But we want different things from life."

"So that means we can't be friends?"

"That's right. I don't want you for my friend, Nick. I have plenty of friends already. I wanted more. I wanted something you can't give."

The elevator arrived, and the doors opened behind her. Quickly, she turned and walked inside. After pushing the button for her floor, she watched Nick as the doors began to close.

"What if I want more, too?" he said. "What if I want you, alone?"

The doors came together with a dull click, and Nick was gone.

Chapter Four

Nick pounded once on the metal elevator doors, then shook his hand out as he cursed. Nothing had gone right. He should have figured as much when she greeted him by getting sick to her stomach.

If he knew what was good for him, he'd turn around, walk to his car and go straight back to his hotel. With luck, he could get a flight to Italy tomorrow. He'd done what he came to do. He'd apologized to her. It was over. *Finito*. She wanted a husband, and he wasn't looking for a wife. That's all. It wasn't a crime that he didn't want to get married. Lots of people didn't. He liked his life just fine the way it was.

He was a free man. He could come and go as he pleased. If he felt like going to Paris for a night, he went. If he wanted to buy something, he bought it. How many married men could say the same thing?

He'd watched his cousins marry, one by one. They all used to play soccer on the weekends. No more. Their wives wanted them home. They used to go to the bistro and drink. No more of that, either. "Wives," he said aloud, making it sound like a dirty word. "Only fools get wives."

He turned, glad to have this ugly episode over, and walked back to the Porsche. She'd want him to get a sensible car. American women all wanted mini-vans. Not him. He would rather die. He opened the door and got in, and cursed again as his head hit the frame. Rubbing the sore spot, he looked back at the elevator door, and this time, he cursed in English.

Finally, the pounding in his head stopped and he slipped the key into the ignition. But there his hand stilled. An image of his cousin Carlo came to him. Carlo with his wife Sophia. He had to admit, Carlo was a new man since he'd found her. He was happy, as happy a man as Nick had ever known. The way he looked at Sophia was something Nick had thought a lot about. There was a contentment in his cousin that made Nick too aware of his own restlessness.

So he had freedom. He also had loneliness. It wasn't so much fun, flying off every week, as it had been in the beginning. Hotel rooms. Packing and unpacking. Restaurants and taxis, and setting his watch. Even the women had started to blur together. Except Jessica.

She was different from all the others. He tried to

figure out why, but there wasn't a specific reason. Her hair, maybe? Soft and beautiful, with all those different shades of red? Her laugh? When she let go, there was no sound like it in the world. Or perhaps it was the way she loved her lists. Those lists. He'd seen one by accident. Pros on one side, cons on the other. The subject had been him. Whether she should go out with him again. The cons had outweighed the pros by quite a bit. She didn't know him. He was too smooth. She wasn't sure if he wanted just sex, or more. And yet she'd gone out with him, anyway. Why?

Then he remembered the pros. It had made him a little nervous, when he'd seen that side of the page. Only two things had been written down. The first—she liked him. That one had been okay. It was the second that had made him sorry he'd seen the list at all. *He makes me feel.* She'd underlined the word *feel* four times.

He looked again at the elevator doors. The truth was, she made *him* feel. He wasn't sure if that was good or bad. But if he left now, he'd never know.

JESSICA NIBBLED ON a cracker as she stared at the television set. Some news program was on, but she wasn't really watching it. She was too busy feeling miserable. Not because she felt sick again, but because of Nick.

Why was she so upset? Her decision had been

completely sound. They wanted different things from life. He was a playboy. He'd never be the kind of husband she wanted or needed. He'd never be any kind of husband!

She really did believe he'd be a good, if infrequent, father. Nick would never abandon any child of his. She laughed, spraying some cracker on her lap. As she wiped her skirt, she realized that Nick might already be a father. Maybe he had children all over the world! Wouldn't that be a kick in the pants.

Once again, she cursed her luck. She'd been so careful, too. They'd used a condom. All three times! She should have done more. She should never had made love with him. It had been irrational. Emotional. Foolish. She'd ignored all her own advice, all her lists, and let her heart lead the way. And here she was—pregnant, nauseous and alone.

Of course, she had Jeff and the other guys at the office. She could just imagine how excited they were going to be about the baby. Like all four of them were going to be the father, instead of Nick. She'd wanted to tell them a hundred times, but she'd held off. It didn't feel right to give them the news before she told Nick. But she could already picture what they'd do. Jeff would want to design the nursery. And what a nursery it would be. He'd go nuts. Pull out all the stops. She smiled. Jeff would be there for her. No matter what.

So would the others. Even Stan. Stan, who acted like the tough guy, but who treated her like a princess. Her boys. Her wonderful boys.

Of all the situations for a single mom to be in, she had it made. So what if she didn't get along with her mother? She had four wonderful friends who were her family now. The baby would be showered with love.

So why did she feel so darn awful? She got up to put the crackers in the kitchen and get ready for bed. The knock on the door startled her so badly she dropped the crackers on the floor. Then her heart started pounding in her chest. What if it was Nick? What if he'd come back, if he'd meant those words he'd shouted in the garage?

No. It was probably Jeff. Or Stan. She left the mess on the floor and went to the door. Standing on tiptoe, she looked through the peep hole. It was Nick. Oh, God.

He knocked again, and she pulled the door open.

"Hello, *cara mia.*"

"Hello."

"May I come in?"

She hesitated, but only for a second. "Okay."

Nick walked past her, and she closed the door behind him. She couldn't believe that her pulse could race like this. It was crazy. Why did she continue to hope for a miracle, when miracles never happened?

"Can I get you something?"

He stepped on the package of crackers, and she quickly bent to pick it up. "Sorry."

"Let me," he said, bending next to her.

They grabbed for the box at the same time, and his hand brushed hers. A jolt went through her, from fingers to toes. He looked up at her, startled. So he'd felt it, too.

His hand moved until he'd covered hers. His gaze never left her own. She grew dizzy, but it was Nick's eyes that threw her off balance. The longing she saw in those dark brown depths.

He leaned toward her, and she knew he was going to kiss her. She should get up. Run. Hide. His kisses were dangerous. They made her forget herself. Forget everything in the world. But she didn't run. She closed her eyes and leaned forward.

The second his lips touched hers, she was a goner. Nick's mouth, Nick's taste, Nick's scent—they all conspired to steal her breath away.

Gently at first, he explored her, running his tongue ever so lightly over her lips, then he wasn't gentle anymore. She moaned as he kissed her hard, deeply, with a passion that woke the most sensitive parts of her body.

His hand went to the back of her neck and held her steady as he lifted her so he could move in closer. Both on their knees, now pressed together, his other hand stole around her waist. She felt him now, his hard chest against her breasts, his stomach, his thighs, and the hard proof that he, too, remembered making love. Remembered how he fit inside her, how their bodies seemed made for each other.

No one had ever kissed her like this. And she'd never responded with such abandon. Her tongue teased, tasted, licked, wanting more and more. When his hand moved from her neck to her breast, she trembled. He knew how to touch her in a way that shot down her defenses, that thrilled her beyond thinking. This man, this father of her—

She broke the kiss, pushing herself back, away. Before he had a chance to protest, she got to her feet, taking the package of crumbled crackers with her.

Not daring to look at him, she went to the kitchen. She heard him get up, but she waited to turn until her breathing became normal and the heat left her cheeks.

"What happened?" he asked, his voice still coarse and low.

"We shouldn't have done that." She faced him but kept her distance. "Why did you come up here, Nick?"

"I don't want this to be the end, Jessica."

"Why not? What is it you want?"

He swiped his hand over his face, then stared

down at the floor as if gathering his thoughts. Finally, he looked back at her, his gaze sober. "I'm not sure. I know, that's not a good answer. You want something concrete, a promise, but I can't give you that. Not because I don't want to. I'd like to say I want the same things you do, but..." He took a step toward her. "I want time, Jessica. Time to know you better. Time to learn what we have."

The urge to just say yes was strong, but that was her heart talking, not her head. Her heart, which had brought her to this place, which had tricked her into believing too much already. She knew enough about Nick to realize he wasn't the man she needed in her life, no matter how much she wanted him. "I don't think that's a very good idea."

"Why not, *cara?*"

"I can't see a happy ending here, Nick. No matter how you slice it, I'll still be me, and you'll still be you."

"What about an us?"

She shook her head. "Us? No, I don't think so. You'll be off somewhere. I'll be here."

"That doesn't mean it can't work. Lots of people spend time apart, but they still—"

"Love each other? Is that what you're saying?"

"I..." He inhaled deeply, then let his breath out slowly. "I don't know. That's why I want the time. To see. I've never been in love, Jessica. Not the kind we're talking about. I don't know what it's like. All I'm sure of is that I don't want to let you go."

"You're asking a lot. More than I'm willing to give."

"I don't understand. I know you care for me. I know it. Jessica, *mi amore,* you came to Rome. You climbed the trellis. It has to mean something."

"It does. I won't deny it. I do care for you, but that's the trouble, don't you see? For you, it's an experiment. If it doesn't work out, you get on your jet and fly away. No big deal."

"No big deal? You underestimate yourself, Jessica. You are a very big deal, indeed."

She shook her head, struggling not to give in. She had to be smart now. So much was at stake. The one thing she knew for sure was that no matter what, Nick wasn't going to change. People didn't change. Maybe he wanted to, but that wasn't enough. Even if he did think he loved her, there would always be that next trip to Paris, or New York, or Athens, and he would find another Gina or Libby. He wouldn't mean to hurt her, but he would. And she would be here, with their child, always wondering. She wouldn't do that to herself, or the baby.

"Please, Jessica. Give me a chance. That's all I'm asking for."

"We had our chance, Nick."

"Oh, no. That one moment? That one trick of

the gods? It was a coincidence, that's all. A one-in-a-million accident.''

''It was a sign. A very big neon sign. I saw the way you looked at Libby and Gina. You cared for them, too, Nick.''

''Not like I feel for you, Jessica.''

''No? You said you loved us all. Remember?''

He sighed. ''Yes. But I came back for you.'' He walked to her, and she instinctively stepped back until the kitchen counter stopped her. He took her arms in his hands and captured her gaze. ''I came back for you, Jessica. Don't send me away before we begin. Take the risk, *cara*.'' He kissed her, once, hard, molding his body to hers, letting her feel his heat and his need. Then he pulled back, but only a little. ''Don't be afraid to *feel*.''

She shook her head and tore herself out of his grasp. ''I am afraid,'' she said. ''I don't want to feel, don't you get it? Because all I end up feeling is hurt. I can't do that, Nick. I won't.''

''I'm taking a risk, too,'' he said softly. ''You're not the only one who has something to lose.''

''It's not the same.''

''Why? You think because I'm a man, I don't get hurt?''

''Not because you're a man. Because you're you.''

''That's not true, Jessica. You don't know me well enough to say that.''

"But I do. You're not the only one who can read people, Nick. I know who you are. You're a man who lives for the moment. Who needs his freedom. Who doesn't want to be held down by anything or anyone. Nick, you're a pilot because you love it. You don't need the money. You fly because it's the fastest getaway car in the world."

"I'm not flying now. I'm right here."

"What about tomorrow?"

"I can't give you any guarantees. Life doesn't work that way."

"I know where I'll be tomorrow. And the next day, and the day after."

"Jessica, life can change in a heartbeat. The only thing you can know with certainty is that it *will* change."

"But there still has to be something you can count on. I can count on my job. My friends. I can count on myself, Nick." She turned away from him, hit suddenly by a wave of nausea so strong she thought she might lose it. Walking quickly to her couch, she steadied herself with one hand while she pressed her stomach with the other.

"What's wrong?" Nick was at her side in an instant.

She shook her head, unable to speak, struggling to regain her equilibrium. She didn't want to lose it now. Not now.

"You're ill. I'll call a doctor."

"No," she said, but that's all she could say.

"You're white like a ghost." He went to the phone and picked it up. "I'm calling an ambulance. Now."

"No, Nick. Don't. I'm okay."

"That is not okay." He kept the phone in his hand as he walked up to her again. He put his other hand on her forehead. "No fever, but you're sweating. Jessica, it could be something serious. Your appendix. I know the symptoms. I've had passengers on my flights who were sick like you. They needed immediate medical attention."

"It's not that." Oh, Lord, she wasn't going to make it. Her stomach lurched again and she ran to the bathroom, slamming the door behind her.

Nick stared at the closed door. If Jessica thought he was going to stand by and do nothing while she could be dying, she was crazy. He had seen this before. A man's appendix had burst on a flight from Italy to New York. He'd nearly died.

He walked over to the bathroom and knocked on the door. "Are you all right?"

He got no response. Well, not in words. What he did hear made him grimace. The only other times he'd seen people sick like this was when the turbulence was terrible. Or sometimes, when women were—

He dropped the phone. Oh, Holy Mother. It

couldn't be. They'd used protection. All three times. "Jessica?"

She didn't answer.

"Jessica!" He couldn't stand it. He had to know. He reached for the doorknob and pushed open the door.

Jessica was at the sink, rinsing her mouth, her toothbrush still in her hand. She was white, pasty white, and her eyes were huge, staring at him for barging in.

"Tell me why you didn't want me to call the doctor."

She didn't speak. But the toothbrush in her hand trembled.

"It's true, then. You're…"

She swallowed.

"We're…"

She stood up straight. Her hand went to her stomach.

He stared at that hand, then slowly let his gaze move up to hers. "Baby?"

She nodded.

"Our baby?"

"Yes."

Nick grabbed for the door, but he didn't make it. The room got too dark, his knees got too weak. And then it went black.

Chapter Five

Jessica rushed over to Nick's prone body and got to her knees. She grabbed his shoulders and shook him. "Nick! Wake up!" He was limp in her arms, his face now matching hers white for white.

She got up again and went to the sink, filling her rinsing glass with cold water. Her hand shook and she spilled a little, but she managed to turn back to him.

Just as his eyes fluttered open, she flung the water square in his face, unable to stop the motion by the time it registered that he was coming to.

The water hit right on target, flying in his eyes, nose and open mouth. He sputtered and coughed, and for a panicky second she thought he might be choking. Then his hand went to his face and he rubbed his eyes. She took in a great breath of air.

"What happened?" he said.

"You fainted."

He sat up, shaking his head. Little droplets of water flew from his wet hair. "I didn't."

"You did."

"Don't be ridiculous. I don't faint."

"So how do you think you got to the ground?" she asked, amazed that he could be so obstinate, despite the evidence.

"I don't know."

He felt the back of his head and looked at her suspiciously. It took her a second to realize he was checking for lumps. She laughed, dumbfounded. "You think I knocked you out?"

"No," he said, but she heard the doubt.

"Nick, you passed out. Cold."

"Why would I do that?"

"You don't remember?"

He shook his head again, then climbed to his feet. "Remember what?"

She didn't want a repeat performance of his swan dive. Taking his hand in hers, she led him back to the living room, maneuvered him to the couch and sat him down. He looked at her as if she might hit him again. That actually might not be such a bad idea.

"You remember that I was sick, right?"

He nodded cautiously.

"That I went to the bathroom in a real hurry."

Again, the slow nod.

"Then you barged in."

His head stopped bobbing. His eyes widened. His face grew pale once more, and she leaned forward ready to catch him, but he didn't pass out. He just gave her this weird look. His lips curved up in a sort of smile. He blinked several times. He cocked his head to the side, and then he said something in Italian that she didn't understand.

"Nick?" She wasn't liking this. Not at all. She couldn't tell if he was happy, in shock, or if he'd just plain lost his marbles.

He leapt up, scaring her to death. She backed away, fast. But he just kept up with her. She backed up even farther and sat in her chair. She wasn't nauseous anymore. Just, well, mystified. It wouldn't have surprised her if Nick suddenly started to crow like a rooster. Perhaps she would call that ambulance now.

"You're pregnant!" he said, shouting the words, waving his hands in the air like a maestro.

"I'm pregnant," she repeated, trying to read him. To get some kind of clue as to what was going on.

"With my child!"

"Yes," she said. "That's right."

"Well, this is…this is…"

"Yes?" Her pulse raced, and for the second time, she held her breath.

"Wonderful!"

She sighed. Maybe all Italian men reacted this way to an unplanned pregnancy. Or maybe Nick

was really nuts. As far as she could see, there
wasn't a whole lot wonderful going on. They'd just
determined that a relationship between them was
impossible. Well, she had. And now he was acting
like he'd been handed good news. Great news.

Nick's smile had changed to one she recognized.
Happy, proud, content. Alarmingly like the smile
he'd given her after that first time they'd made love.
It must be a male thing. He Tarzan, she a very
knocked-up Jane. Didn't he realize how complicated this made their lives?

"When are we due?"

"I don't know about you, but I'm due in eight
months."

"A boy. You think it will be a boy?"

"That's not exactly the hot issue on the table.
We have some things to discuss."

"Right," he said. "But first, champagne. You
have any?"

"No, I don't have any champagne."

"I'll go get some. Champagne. To celebrate."
He reached into his pocket for his keys and headed
for the door.

"Nick," she said.

He reached for the knob.

"Nick!"

He turned. "Yes?"

"No champagne."

His brows furrowed. "But this is important."

"First, I can't drink. I'm pregnant."

He opened his mouth, then shut it again. "Oh, yes."

"Second, we need to talk."

He looked at her for a long minute, then nodded. As he walked back toward her, she could see the balloon of his elation deflate. She was sorry to rain on his parade, but for heaven's sake!

He sat down in the chair across from her. "So, we talk."

She needed to regroup. Never in her wildest imagination had she expected Nick to react with such glee. She'd prepared for anger, for coldness, for resignation. Not for this. She didn't understand it. Was he this happy because she was carrying his baby? Or was it just that he'd fathered a child?

"Jessica?"

She'd been staring. Now was her chance to talk to him, but she didn't have any idea where to start. Damn it, this was all too fast! She needed time to prepare. Why was it Nick always seemed to take her by surprise? But she had to start somewhere. "I'll go get my things," she said.

He looked at her, confusion creasing his brow. "What things?"

She stood. "Just wait here."

While Jessica went to her bedroom, Nick let his thoughts wander. A baby! He was going to be a father. It was so easy to see his son at five or six.

Dark haired, like him. Tall, like all the Carluccis. Maybe even his smile. He'd love the villa, just as much as Nick had loved growing up there. All those rooms to explore. The banisters to slide down. Mama would be so pleased. How she had been after him to have an heir. Someone to carry on the name. And Theresa! She'd finally be quiet about him growing up. He was going to be a father. Amazing.

"Come," Jessica said as she walked back into the room. "I think we can see these better in here."

He turned as she headed toward the dining room. She carried a large poster board, piled with books and papers. He got up to follow.

She put her things on the table, then went to the corner and brought out an easel. Motioning him to a chair, she pulled out the poster board and placed it upright.

It was a chart. A gestational chart. With pictures. Divided by months. Each picture represented a stage of development, from a tiny squiggle to a very good rendition of a curled-up baby. Underneath each picture was a list of symptoms. Below the symptoms were lists of questions.

He laughed. Laughed so hard, tears came to his eyes. It was so…so…Jessica!

"What's so funny?"

He coughed and brought himself under control. When he looked at her, he could see he'd upset her.

"I'm sorry, *cara mia,* but I wasn't expecting this."
He nodded toward the chart.

"It's very informational. And well researched."

"I'm sure it is, darling."

"Don't patronize me, Nick. This is important.
We have someone's life at stake here. We can't
afford to take any chances."

"Of course not."

"Okay, then." She turned to the chart and
pointed at the littlest squiggle. "That's where we
are now," she said. "I've been to the obstetrician,
of course. I'm taking prenatal vitamins already. My
diet is good, and I've found a gym where they have
classes for pregnant women...."

Nick listened to her go on about her preparations,
but only with half an ear. He knew Jessica well
enough to know she needed to play with her charts
and graphs, that they gave her a sense of control.
It wasn't necessary for him to remind her that
women had been having babies for centuries, and
that she had no more control over matters than a
peasant woman in Sicily. But he couldn't concentrate. Not when his thoughts were so wild in his
head. He had to call home. Mama needed to hear
this news soon. Then he needed to call the airline
and take a longer leave of absence. There was much
to be done here before he could go back to work.

But the details, he didn't need to think of those.
He would leave those to Jessica. She liked her de-

tails, and he didn't want to take that pleasure from her.

Maybe the boy would have Jessica's eyes. He hoped so. They were so very beautiful. And some of her logic. Not all of it. He would need some of his papa's imagination. But Jessie had good sense. He'd want that for his son.

His son. The idea made him giddy. He'd never thought much about having a child. Not seriously. Just that someday, if he settled down, he would have bambinos. But now that it was here, he liked this idea very much. He also liked the fact that the mama was going to be Jessica. Fate was very, very kind.

"And according to most of the literature, this morning sickness of mine should last only another month. But there is a chance it'll go longer. God, I hope not."

He couldn't sit anymore. He went to her, took the pencil from her hand and put it on the table. Then he took her and wrapped her in his arms. "I'm very pleased, Jessica."

She laid her head upon his chest, and he felt her sigh. "I gathered."

"But you don't sound so happy."

"It's complicated."

"Why?"

She pulled back, looking at him as if he were crazy. "Why? Are you serious?"

"We'll work everything out. It will be all right, *cara*. I promise."

"I don't understand you. I really don't."

She started to turn away from him, but he caught her. When she didn't look at him, he touched her chin to bring her gaze to his. The look in her eyes worried him. She really was confused. Unsettled. "I know it's not what we planned, but it's still a blessing, no? A little baby," he said as he reached down to touch her stomach. "Our little baby."

"It's not a toy we're talking about here. This little baby will grow up. There'll be school, doctors, child care. There are a million things that could go wrong, Nick. I've never been around children. Ever. I never baby-sat, none of my friends have kids. What if I screw it up?"

"You?"

She nodded, and he saw her eyes grow moist with tears. He pulled her close once more, angry at himself for not realizing she'd be so scared. It never occurred to him, not with Jessica. She was so strong. So smart. "Jessica?"

She nodded on his chest.

"No child could wish for a better mother. Whatever happens, you'll be ready. You'll handle it. We'll handle it."

"Will we?"

"Yes. Together."

"But..."

"Shhh. No more worries. Not tonight. Tonight is for joy. For celebration. Tomorrow is time enough to worry."

She sighed again, and he felt her muscles relax.

"Now, how about that dinner? So we can't have champagne. We can toast our luck with sparkling water."

Once more, she pulled back. "I don't think I can," she said. "I'm awfully tired."

He studied her face. She'd never really gotten her color back. "Of course. But you should eat."

"I'll have some soup a little later."

"I can cook that for you."

"No, thank you. I think I just want to rest for a bit."

He didn't want to leave her. But there were those phone calls. And she did look like some sleep would do her good. He leaned forward and kissed her gently. "Tomorrow, we celebrate, eh?"

She nodded. "Sure."

He looked at her for another moment. The mother of his child. So beautiful. Of all the women in the world, he was glad this had happened with Jessica.

SLEEP WOULDN'T COME. She'd been in bed for two hours, but her brain wouldn't stop spinning. She kept thinking about Nick's reaction. His unabashed happiness. His complete lack of understanding.

How could he not realize how complicated this was? He lived in Rome. When he was home, that is. Most of the time he was somewhere else. Sure, he came to Los Angeles, but not that often. The lion's share of responsibility for the baby was going to be hers. She'd be the one to get up nights, to make all the hundreds of daily decisions, to cope with any problems that came up.

Nick would undoubtedly want her and the baby to come to Rome. That would completely disrupt their lives. What about work? What about—

Oh, this wasn't the way it was supposed to be. She turned over and hugged her pillow. All her life, she'd imagined the day she'd get pregnant. But in her dreams, she was married. To a man who loved her. Whom she loved in return. They lived in the same city. Certainly the same country.

Her life was turning out all wrong. All because of one mistake. All because she'd listened to her heart. Now it was happening again. This traitorous heart of hers was telling her sweet lies. That Nick wanted to marry her. That she and the baby would be so important to him that he'd give up his precious flying.

That he loved her, not just the child they'd created.

For the first time in five years, Jessica wept.

Chapter Six

Jessica finished the budget for the Wilkins's house and saved it on her computer. Yawning yet again, she wished that caffeine wasn't on her list of no-nos. The herbal tea just wasn't cutting it after her sleepless night.

A knock on her office door made her turn. Jeff walked in without preamble. "How are you this morning, sunshine?" he asked as he plopped himself into her big club chair. "I hope you feel better than you look."

"Thanks so much."

"If you won't get the colonic, then you have to do vitamins. I can set you up with my nutritionist this afternoon. She'll get rid of that bug you've got in a minute. I tell you, she's a miracle worker."

"I already take vitamins, Jeffrey, but thank you just the same."

"Jessie, girl, you are more stubborn than Paul's cowlick, and honey, *that's* stubborn."

"It's just one of the things that makes me special," she said, smiling brightly.

Jeff grunted.

She laughed, but then that's what Jeff did. He had a knack for making her laugh. One of the best designers in the country, he wasn't at all the pretentious snob he could have been. According to Paul, the youngest and most recent addition to the firm, Jeff was hurting business by not living up to the stereotype. But Jeff wouldn't be Jeff if he did anything that wasn't completely true to his nature. Good hearted, generous, he was the complete opposite of a prima donna. Despite Paul's conviction, their client list was as healthy as she could have hoped for.

It didn't hurt that Jeff was also gorgeous. At six foot six, his body was a living testament to the benefits of a personal trainer. Blond and blue-eyed, he had once, briefly, been a model, and for good reason. But again, he didn't let his good looks go to his head. Pursued by men and women on a daily basis, he and his partner had been together for eight years. It was the healthiest relationship Jessica had ever seen.

"So what's on your agenda today, sweetheart?" Jeff asked.

"Nothing glamorous. Just another budget, some phone calls and banking."

"Yech," he said. "Sounds like you need a great lunch to counteract all that tedium."

"Just because you don't have the use of your left brain, doesn't mean that I don't."

"And I admire you terribly for it, but that doesn't negate the fact that accounting is boring as sh—"

"Jeff, go design something, will you?"

"Not until you tell me you'll come with me to lunch. I'm worried about you, pumpkin. You don't look good."

She thought about just telling him the truth. But the other guys would be furious if they found out she'd spilled the beans to Jeff first. The announcement would have to be made when everyone was present and accounted for. "Not today, okay? Tomorrow, maybe."

He scowled at her, but then he got up and went to the door. "Will you at least go to your own damn doctor?" he said.

She nodded. "It's a promise."

"I mean this week. Not next year."

She crossed her heart.

"Okay, then."

She picked up her mug, but suddenly tea didn't appeal. Nothing much did. What she needed was sleep, and some time to herself. Time to get her thoughts together. To figure out the wisest course of action for her and for the baby. But she wasn't going to get that. If she knew Nick, he'd be leaving town soon, and she wanted to get as much settled before he left as she could. His euphoria had surely lessened overnight. He'd undoubtedly realized that their having a baby wasn't exactly a dream come true for either of them. She also hoped he realized that it wasn't a disaster, either, just a little complicated.

As for her, she'd had to keep reminding herself that Nick had not proposed. He'd not declared his love for her. In fact, not one thing had changed. The best thing that could happen was for Nick to leave so she could get over him once and for all. Only then could this crazy situation have a happy ending. They'd be friends, and it wouldn't break her heart each time she had to talk to him.

Jessica opened her briefcase and pulled out the yellow pad she'd worked on last night. She'd listed all the possible scenarios for her, Nick and the baby. Her first choice was to keep the child here, and for Nick to set up regular visitation schedules. In addition, when the baby was older, she'd take one trip to Rome a year. She wouldn't want to deprive her baby of its Italian heritage, after all.

Second choice was for Nick to visit when he could. She wasn't crazy about the idea of him dropping by whenever, but it wasn't a deal breaker.

After that, it got tricky. He could insist the baby spend more time in Rome. He could—

"*Buon giorno,* Jessica."

She spun around in her chair. Nick stood in her doorway, smiling that same wacky smile he'd worn yesterday. Her chest tightened and she could feel her heart pound, as if that smile were meant for her instead of the baby. It was foolish, but at least she knew what was going on. Her heart and her mind had completely different agendas. One to be trusted, the other to be tolerated until she could figure out how to deal with it.

But it wasn't easy. The fluttering in her tummy wasn't morning sickness. It was Nick sickness. The heat on her cheeks was very real, even though it wasn't logical. And her desire to run to his arms was hard to resist. Too hard.

As he came toward her, she noticed the package in his arms. It was wrapped in pretty blue paper, all tied with a bow. She couldn't stop her smile.

"You look beautiful, *angelo mio*. I hope this means you're feeling beautiful, too?"

She nodded. "I'm better today, thank you." Her gaze kept slipping to his gift.

"Yes," he said, holding it out to her. "It's for you."

Eagerly, she took it from him. She loved presents. She hadn't received a lot of them in her life, and although it wasn't dignified, and totally unlike her usual self, she couldn't help tearing the paper in her haste to see what was inside.

Nick laughed, but she didn't care. Maybe it was

the child inside her that made her toss the wrapping to the floor, rip the tape, fling the box top to her desk. But then she slowed to peel back the tissue.

The sleep shirt was blue, very pale, very pretty. And so tiny it was hard to comprehend that it would fit on a real live baby instead of a doll. She lifted it carefully, marveling at the softness, the workmanship. Then she saw the little booties.

The lump in her throat made it hard to swallow. She felt astonishingly touched, and at the same time a little scared. It was all real, wasn't it? She was actually going to have a baby. Nick's baby.

"You like?"

She nodded, unable to speak for the moment. Her fingers caressed the miniature slippers, while her gaze went to Nick.

He beamed at her. His dark eyes filled with a happiness so unguarded she felt like a voyeur. If only that happiness were for her…No. She wasn't going to go there. *"Grazie,"* she said, her voice a little shaky.

He leaned down and kissed her very softly on the lips. *"Prego,"* he whispered.

"What's all this?"

Jessica leaned sideways as Nick stood up and turned toward her door. "You remember Alan and Jeff, don't you, Nick?"

He nodded and held out his hand. Alan, Jeff's assistant, took it, while his boss looked right at Jessica. He eyed her, indicating Nick, and she smiled at him, then mouthed, "It's okay."

Jeff's gaze went to the booties in her hand. "Who's having a baby?"

Before Jessica could say anything, Nick said, "We are. Hasn't she told you?"

The silence in the room was thunderous. Jessica stared at Jeff, then Alan, then glared at Nick. His eyes widened with disbelief. "You didn't tell them?"

"No, Nick. Not yet."

"You're kidding, right?" Jeff said. "You're *pregnant?*"

Jessica nodded. "Yep."

"And you didn't tell us?" He was shouting now, and Jessica kind of shrunk in her chair.

Alan, who still had Nick's hand in his, finally came out of his daze. "I simply do not believe this. Jess, you slay me. You absolutely slay me. Keeping this a secret? From us? Does Paul know? I have to tell Paul."

"Paul does not know, and neither does Stan," Jessica said as she reached for her phone. She dialed Stan's extension and asked him to come in, and to bring Paul.

"So when did this happen?" Jeff asked. "I thought you two broke up in Rome?"

Nick waved that away as he came back to stand

next to her. "It was a silly misunderstanding. Unimportant. Now we have the baby to think about."

Jeff continued to stare at her, one brow raised ominously. "You and I are going to have a talk later, young lady."

She nodded. "I know. I'm sorry I didn't say anything before."

"I'm going to forgive you," he said. "But only because I'm a goddamned sweetheart."

She reached up and squeezed his hand. "Yes, you are."

"Wow, Jess," Alan said, shaking his head as he lifted the package from her lap. "How far along are you?"

This wasn't going at all the way she'd planned. She'd wanted to wait, at least past the first trimester. So much could happen in the next couple of months. First Nick finds out, then the guys. Wasn't anything going to go her way?

"A month," Nick said. "A little more than that."

"What's up?"

Jessica turned to see Stan and Paul come in. Stan, her gruff guardian, was the one she was worried about. He was the architect for the firm, and he kept himself a little separate from the others. Oh, they were all pretty close, but she'd always known that Stan rarely confided in anyone but her. She hadn't wanted him to find out this way.

"Booties?"

Her gaze moved to Paul, who was gazing at the tiny slippers in wonder.

"Guess who's knocked up?" Alan said.

"And who didn't think it was important enough to share with her best friends," Jeff added.

"Jessie?" Paul's surprise made his voice crack a little, but Jessica's gaze stayed on Stan. He looked at her hard, and she nodded, then gave him an apologetic smile.

"It's true. Not the part that Jeff said. I was going to tell you all, but..."

"But you didn't," Stan said, finishing for her.

"Who's the father?" Paul asked, staring at Nick. They hadn't met on Nick's last visit.

"I'm Nick Carlucci," Nick said, holding out his hand to Paul. "Proud papa."

"Nick from Rome? But I thought you two were history."

"Update," Alan said. "It was a misunderstanding. Now everything's just peachy."

"Well, all I can say is it's a good thing you didn't wait any longer to tell us. It's going to take every day we have to get a nursery together for you." Jeff walked over to the couch and flung himself down. "I don't suppose you'll move to a bigger place, will you?"

"No, of course not," Jessica said. "I like where

I live, and we don't need to do much. The baby can stay in the second bedroom."

"And where will you move your desk? The file cabinets? No, sweet cheeks. Not a chance. We're going to have to change everything."

"You know," Alan said, "if we knocked out that wall between the second bedroom and the living room, we could make the space work." He grabbed a yellow pad and pen from her desk and went to sit next to Jeff.

Nick looked at Jessica, questioningly.

"It's no use talking to them. I knew they would be this way. They're going to do up a nursery whether I like it or not. I won't let them knock down any walls, but we don't have to tell them that yet."

"I see," he said.

Jessica doubted it. By now, all four guys were huddled at the couch, each tossing suggestions into the pot. Alan sketched furiously, and Paul took notes. Only Stan hesitated for a moment to look at her.

"They're my friends," Jessica said softly to Nick. "My family."

"Speaking of family..." Nick spied a chair in the corner and pulled it next to her. He reached over and turned her chair until they were facing each other. "I told Mama. And Theresa."

"Oh, dear."

"No, they were thrilled. Mama cried."

"That's good?"

"That's good. It will be her first grandchild. She thought it would never happen." He shook his head. "I can't tell you how much she wanted this. She went to the church to light candles and thank St. Joseph."

"I'm glad. But you know, it's a little soon for everyone to be so excited. I mean, what if something happens?"

"Nothing will happen. I have very strong genes." He reached over and touched her stomach. "This one is perfect. I know. A perfect boy."

"Oh?"

He shrugged. "Or girl. But I don't think so. Mama will tell us for sure."

"She will?"

"She knows these things. Each of my cousins, when she rubbed the bellies, she knew."

"Nick, I don't know when I'm going to go back to Rome. I have work, and new expenses—"

"Rome? She's coming here. With Theresa."

"What?"

"Of course! This is her first grandchild. And she's never met you."

Jessica's stomach constricted, but good. Nick's mother? Here? His sister? She looked at the couch, listening as her friends argued over the nursery. It was all too much. Too fast. None of this was in her plans. None of this was her life.

"I don't care, it's not going to work," Jeff said, so loudly, Jessica had to look. "She has to move and that's final."

Nick looked, too. "What's that? What's not going to work?" He got up and walked over to the boys.

"Her apartment is too small," Alan said. "She'd have to give up her office altogether, and even then, there wouldn't be enough room. For heaven's sake, she lives in a shoe box."

Nick looked over at the yellow pad but gave that up quickly. "Of course she'll move," he said, switching his attention to Paul's notes. "We'll find a house. Not an apartment. A big house with plenty of room for the baby."

Jessica couldn't believe what she was hearing. What the hell was happening here? This was her baby. Her life. Nick's mother was coming, and now he wanted her to move? Saying it as if she had no vote?

"I know this fabulous house," Paul said. "Five blocks from the beach. Great guest quarters. Maid's room, too. It's pricey, but worth every dime. If I had the money, I'd snap it up in a heartbeat."

"There's that big one up on Sunset, too," Stan said. "I could really do something with that."

"You don't have a lot of time," Jeff said. "If

you want us to get everything ready in eight months.''

"Okay.'' Nick nodded.

"Wait just a darn minute,'' Jessica said, getting madder by the moment.

No one turned. Not one of them.

"We'll look at houses soon,'' Nick said. "But first, we have to find a church.''

"A church?'' Jessica said. "Would you please listen? Hello! The one having the baby is talking.''

"What kind?'' Alan asked, ignoring her.

"Catholic, of course. For the wedding.''

Chapter Seven

Jessica couldn't move. Or speak. Or breathe. Had she just heard Nick say he wanted to marry her? No. He hadn't said that. He'd said they were going to be married. No asking. No proposal. No discussion. Just bingo. Done deal. *Finito.*

She didn't think it was a joke. None of the guys were laughing. They hadn't even paused in their conversation. As if it was no biggie. As if it was a given.

Was she insane? Hadn't she just been bemoaning the fact that Nick hadn't said anything about marriage? So why did she feel so outraged? So manipulated?

"Nick?" He didn't hear her. *"Nick!"*

He turned to her with a smile. "Yes, *carissima?*"

"Can I speak to you?"

He glanced once more at Paul's list, then came back over to her desk. "Are you all right?"

"No, I'm not."

His smile vanished, replaced with a genuine look of concern, which didn't make her feel better. She didn't believe the concern was for her. Just for the mother of his child.

"What is it? Are you feeling sick again? Can I get you something?"

"You can explain what you were talking about a minute ago."

"The house? I want you to be happy, Jessica. To have a beautiful home. With a wonderful nursery. I myself remember my nursery at the villa. I had a—" his brows came together for a moment as if he were searching for the right word "—nanny there. So kind. So loving. We'll find little Nicolo a nanny like that, eh?"

"Little Nicolo?"

He laughed. "We can discuss the name."

"That's not all we need to discuss."

"What do you mean?"

"The house. The nanny. The nursery. The wedding."

"Yes?"

Was he really this dense? He honestly looked confused. Jessica shook her head in amazement. "Didn't it occur to you that I might have an opinion about those things? That you might have asked me before you made all those decisions about my life?"

"You don't want a new house?"

"No. I don't."

"Why not?"

"Nick, that's not the point. I don't want you waltzing in here making decisions for me. Just because I'm having your kid, doesn't mean I'm handing over my life."

His right brow rose. The corners of his mouth lifted slightly. Smugly.

Jessica suddenly realized the room was quiet. She looked over at the couch. All four men had grown still and were watching her and Nick as if they were on an episode of "The Guiding Light."

"Don't you people have work to do?" she said.

"Yeah, but this is more interesting," Jeff said, winking at her.

"Don't you wink at me. You get out of here, right now. Take your pads and your drawings and scram. Got it?"

Paul stood up immediately. But then, he was new. The rest of them took their own sweet time. The looks Jeff and Alan gave Nick didn't escape her. Conspiratorial. Deprecating. Bemused. She wanted to line them all up in a row and slap them one at a time. Well, all except Stan. Although he had been a willing participant in this mess, he wasn't sharing the joke with the others.

Matter of fact, he walked over to her, right between her and Nick, and took hold of her shoulders. "You stick to your guns, Jess, you hear me?"

"I'm trying. But I'm slightly outnumbered."

He smiled. "You know they love you. They only want what's best."

"They know that, then? What's best for me?"

He didn't say anything for a minute. Then he gave her a crooked smile. "Maybe not. But the color scheme will work, no matter what."

"That's a big comfort, thanks."

He leaned over and kissed her on the cheek. She smiled, grateful he'd diffused some of her anger so she could think a little more rationally. Then he let her go and turned to Nick.

"You be good to her, you hear me?"

Nick nodded. "I give you my word."

"Okay, then." Stan jerked his head at the guys. "Let's go."

Everyone left the office, all of them looking back at least once at the soap opera that was becoming Jessica's life. Finally, she and Nick were alone.

"These friends of yours," Nick said. "They care a great deal about you."

"Yes, they do. Although they sometimes forget that I'm a grown woman. That I have a mind of my own, and I'm perfectly capable of handling my own life."

"So," he said, taking her arm and leading her to the couch. "You want to discuss? We'll discuss."

"Thank you," she said. She sat down, and he sat right next to her.

He took her hand in his, brought it to his lips and kissed her palm gently. It didn't seem to matter that she was still angry as hell, the little gesture made her stomach flutter. That wasn't fair. She extracted her hand and put it in her lap.

"Tell me what's wrong, *cara mia.*"

"What's wrong is that this is all going too fast."

"What?"

"Everything. The baby. You. Your mother."

"You're worried about Mama? She's going to love you. Trust me."

"I'm not worried about that. Well, yes I am, but that's not it. Nick, I don't know what I want. Not yet. It's too soon. I'm still getting used to the idea that I'm really pregnant."

"Yes, I see."

"I don't think you do. I don't think you've thought this through. We don't really even know each other, and you're talking about houses and weddings."

"You don't want the baby to have a father?"

She heard the slight shock in his tone. It shouldn't have surprised her, but it did. After all, he was Italian. And even though he was as worldly and debonair a man as she'd ever met, he was still old-fashioned. "The baby has a father. Whether we're married or not."

Nick looked at her with real hurt in his eyes. "My family is old, Jessica. Proud. We have traditions and duties. The villa, it goes back hundreds of years. Back to before the Trevi was built. Back to the time of the Medicis. My son has that history in his blood.''

''I'm not trying to take that away, Nick. But there's more to consider than traditions.''

''What could be more important than that?''

''A stable home. A mother and father who'll be there for him when he needs them.''

''But of course,'' he said. ''That's why I want to get you a house here, in America. So he'll have his home here, and in Rome. That's why we need to marry. So he'll have his mama and papa. Family. Tradition. Isn't that what you want, too?''

''Yes, I want those things, but I don't want to be railroaded.''

''What does that mean?''

''It means I count. It means we have to talk about things that will impact my life before you go making unilateral decisions.''

He nodded. ''I just want what's best for you, *mi amore*.''

''For me? Or for your baby?''

Again, he gave her that bewildered look. Again, she realized they were practically strangers. ''Nick, we need to slow things down. We need to get to know each other. This is all happening too fast.''

He took her hand in his. ''I already know you,

my Jessica. You are the woman on my balcony. In her torn stockings.''

A quick lump formed in her throat. ''I was only that woman for a moment, Nick. I don't know if I can be her ever again.''

NICK SIPPED HIS cappuccino and stared at the yellow pad on the table in front of him. So far, he'd written and scratched out three cons. First, that he and Jessica didn't know each other well. Second, that he was a pilot. Third, that he hadn't planned on getting married.

After careful consideration of each con, he'd turned it to a pro. That he and Jessica were nearly strangers wasn't a bad thing. He had instincts about people, and since the first moment he'd met her, he'd realized she was something special. Hadn't he come all the way to America to apologize to her? They'd get to know each other, to care for each other. It wasn't so many years ago that all marriages started off with strangers. His own grandparents' marriage had been arranged, and that had turned out very happily.

His being a pilot wasn't a negative, either. He'd certainly never overstay his welcome. Jessica wouldn't grow bored of him, and each time he saw her it would be like discovering her all over again. No, that was a plus.

As for him not wanting to wed, well, that had

been a little harder to cross out. Granted, it wasn't a *real* marriage, not like Theresa's would be, but it would change things for both him and Jessica. When he came to America, he would have a home, not a hotel. He would have a child. He would be responsible for two more lives. And there wouldn't be any more American women. Or *any* women.

The problem was, he wasn't sure he could do it. Being with one woman was new territory for him. It wasn't as if he'd been with hundreds of women. But he'd never been with just one. Not for any length of time. Certainly not for a lifetime.

Frankly, he was scared. But he had a duty, and he would perform that duty to the best of his ability. He owed that to his child and his future wife. But being a husband? A father? That prospect had always seemed so far in the future. Good for his cousins, not for him. Didn't they all say how much they envied his life-style? His freedom? And here he was, giving it away.

He looked at the pad again. These lists Jessica liked so much...he didn't see it. He took the top sheet, tore it off and crumpled it into a ball. Sometimes it was better just to do something, not think about it so much.

Nick noticed the waitress heading his way. He also noticed her smile. She was young, early twenties, blond, pretty, a little too thin. She walked toward him, swaying her hips, seeking his gaze. It was a familiar dance, one he knew the steps to very well. If circumstances had been different, he would have smiled back.

"Can I get you something else?" the waitress asked, her voice a smoky invitation.

He shook his head. "Just the check, please."

"I couldn't help but notice your accent. Are you from France?"

He grinned. "Close. Italy."

"Really? I love spaghetti."

Nick pulled out his wallet and handed her a five dollar bill. "I love spaghetti, too," he said, careful to let her know that pasta was the only topic he cared to discuss.

She got the point and, with a little shrug, went off to get him his change.

Nick watched her walk away. The exchange hadn't been unusual. Sometimes started by him, sometimes by the lady. There was that one moment, before words had been spoken, just after eye contact. That one breathless moment when he wasn't sure. When all that existed were possibilities. That's what he would miss. Not what came after.

He thought about Jessica, about that first moment when he'd seen her at the party. He hadn't known many people there, just the hostess and her boyfriend. Jessica had been standing by the fireplace, sipping a glass of champagne. She was listening to a man talk, but not really hearing. He could tell from across the room that she was bored.

He'd been drawn to her immediately. With that dark red hair, her slender but curvy figure in that black suit with the short skirt. Of course she was beautiful, but that's not what had made him cross the room. There had been a surprising number of beautiful women at that party, as he recalled. But Jessica...

What was it? What was it about her that had made him oblivious to every other person in the room? He didn't think it was her looks, but he couldn't put his finger on anything else. What he did remember was the feeling he'd had walking across that room. The anticipation had been so strong, so powerful, that he'd known before he spoke to her that they would be together. That something important was about to occur.

He chuckled to himself, just as the waitress came back with his money. She looked hopeful for another second, but that ended when she saw his face. He got up, leaving her a very generous tip.

As he went to his car, he realized that since that moment, since that first time he'd seen Jessica, he hadn't approached another woman. He'd met Gina and Libby before Jessica, that's right. And after? There had been opportunities, just like with the waitress, but no interest on his part.

All the women he'd met simply weren't Jessica.

If he had to get married at all, he was glad it was to be with her.

HE WAS DUE ANY MOMENT. Jessica wasn't ready. To call this a bad hair day was to do a disservice to all other bad hair days. Nothing worked. Her makeup, the same makeup she'd worn for years, suddenly made her look like a mannequin. Her dress, a favorite, and the fifth one she'd tried on, didn't seem to fit right. It wasn't exactly tight, it just didn't hang properly. And her hair. Well, it was clear she was going to have to go hat shopping if this was what pregnancy did for her.

She grabbed a large barrette and pulled her hair back. Anything else was just an exercise in futility.

Glancing at her watch, she saw that another ten minutes had passed. She'd been getting ready to see Nick for more than two hours. What was with her? For heaven's sake, she'd gotten ready for her prom in forty-five minutes! This wasn't even a date, just dinner. Just a conversation. Just her future.

She put her hand on her stomach, willing the butterflies, if that's all that was, to settle down. Taking in a deep breath, she held it for five counts, then slowly let it out. It didn't help. She was still a wreck.

Ever since he'd left her office this morning, she hadn't been able to think clearly. She could still hardly believe all that had taken place in the last few days. Her whole life had taken a sharp right turn, and she didn't have her seat belt on. Nothing made sense. No easy answers were at hand. She felt helpless, worried and just plain confused.

She thought about talking things over with Jeff but decided against it. He was a dear friend, and a wonderful sounding board, but he was also a guy. What she needed was a woman to talk to. Someone who'd been faced with a situation like this, and had made good choices. Someone who knew her and cared about what happened to her. Which eliminated her mother.

Well, maybe she wasn't being fair. So they didn't have a warm, fuzzy relationship. Mona had been in this situation. She'd gotten pregnant just after high school. She'd decided against marriage, and although Jessica had asked her why many times, her mother had never given her a straight answer.

Maybe now, when she was in the same predicament, her mother would open up? Confide in her?

Jessica checked the time as she went to the phone. Nick wasn't due just yet. And if he did arrive early, she'd ask him to wait. Making the call felt right.

She found her address book and looked up the number. Mona would have left the salon by now. Jessica did another round of deep breathing as she dialed.

"Hello?"

"Mona?"

"Jess. Hi. How are you?"

Immediately, Jessica's stomach tightened. This had been a mistake. "I'm okay," she said. "Well, sort of."

"What's wrong?"

She paused. "I'm pregnant."

Her mother laughed. It wasn't a very good sound. "Well, I'll be damned."

"What does that mean?"

"Nothing. Who's the father?"

"His name is Nick Carlucci. He's from Italy. A pilot."

"Really? Any plans to get married? Or is this going to be a solo effort?"

"I don't know," Jessica said, picturing her mother's cool blue eyes, her carefully tended red hair. The set of her mouth.

"I'm assuming it wasn't planned."

"No, it wasn't. That's why I thought…"

"How far along are you?"

"A month."

"Well, there's still time."

Jessica closed her eyes. "Time for what?"

"To end it. You're still young, Jessica. For God's sake, why take on a burden like that if you don't have to?"

Jessica felt sick. "Look, Mona, I have to go. I just wanted you to know, that's all."

"Well, I appreciate the call. Let me know what you decide."

"I will. Bye, Mona." She replaced the phone on the cradle and made her way to the couch. She thought about getting some crackers, but she didn't want to move. She didn't want to do much of anything.

Damn it, she should have known better. Where was her judgment? Her good sense? How on earth had she ever believed, even for a second, that Mona would be there for her? That anyone would?

She rubbed her stomach gently, trying to quell the unease. When the knock on the door came, she jumped. The room had grown darker, colder. She shivered, then got up to let Nick in.

He stood in her doorway holding a bouquet of mixed flowers. His smile, bright, cheerful, held nothing but confidence. But the smile faded quickly. "What's wrong?" he said, stepping past her into the apartment.

"Nothing," she said.

"No, something is wrong. Are you feeling sick again?"

She closed the door and pasted a smile on her face. "Just a little," she said.

He looked at her for a long while. She wished he wouldn't. Nick had a way of seeing too much. She held her hand out for the flowers, needing the distraction. But he didn't hand them to her.

"Aren't those for me?"

He nodded. "They can wait. First, tell me what happened."

"Nothing happened, Nick. I'm fine."

"Ah, my Jessica. You can't hide from me, don't you know that yet?" He tossed the bouquet on the sofa and moved toward her, seeking out her gaze. "I have seen you fine, *mi amore*. And right now, you aren't fine."

She stepped back, but he stopped her with his hand on her arm. Then he moved his fingers to her face and gently, softly caressed her cheek.

"You're not alone, *cara*."

She wanted to believe him. Even as she fell into his arms, even as the tears wet his shoulder, she wanted to believe him.

Chapter Eight

Nick wrapped his arms tightly around Jessica, the feel of her trembling stirring his blood. Whatever was wrong, he would fix it. Whatever it took. The overwhelming need to protect her was something completely new to him, and so powerful it frightened him.

She sniffed and pulled back. Reluctantly, he let her go.

"I'm sorry," she said. "I didn't mean to do that."

"To come to me when you're sad? You should do that. Always."

Jessica shook her head, then wiped underneath her eyes as if to get rid of any trace of her tears. "It's no big deal," she said. "Certainly not worth crying about. I don't know what's come over me."

"*Ormones,*" he said. "The baby."

She nodded, turning toward the kitchen. "I'm

sure that's it—hormones. Can I get you something to drink?''

"No. But you can tell me what happened.''

"Nothing. Really. Let me get a vase for those flowers. They're really lovely. Thank you.''

He watched her get the vase down from her cupboard and fill it with water while he debated. Should he press her? Should he let it go? What would Carlo do? Nick remembered when his cousin's wife was pregnant. She'd cried all the time. Food—that's it. When she got upset, Carlo would get her something to eat. Sweet things, sour things. That always calmed her down. "You want to go to dinner now?" he asked Jessica.

She put the flowers on the dining room table and adjusted the arrangement. "Okay," she said. "I need to fix my makeup, then we can go.''

"You look beautiful,'' Nick said, startled to realize he meant it. She did, though. Soft and vulnerable, with that little trace of mascara still on her cheek and her normally perfect hair a little fuzzy around her face. There was something unguarded and open about her now that he'd never seen before. He liked that Jessica was a strong woman, that she had her own mind and strong opinions. But this side of her appealed to him in a completely different way. If he thought she'd let him, he would have taken her once more in his arms. But from the way she wouldn't look at him, he knew she would just chase him away.

"Make yourself comfortable," she said as she walked to the bathroom.

He nodded, still troubled, still feeling like there was something he should do. When she left the door open to the bathroom, he decided he would be comfortable watching her, not sitting alone. But he moved quietly. He didn't want to upset her again.

He went toward the bathroom and leaned against the wall just outside. From there he could see her as she took the damp washcloth and wiped her face. His gaze moved down her body, and he tried to picture her in a few months, swollen with their child. He smiled. She would be beautiful then, too. If she were anything like Carlo's wife, she'd become rounder all over. Her cheeks would fill out a bit, and her breasts… They would get big and full.

The thought aroused him. It would be something to see her naked then. When she was her most womanly. He'd never thought about making love to a pregnant woman, but he wanted to with Jessica. The idea was very erotic to him, so much he felt himself harden.

She was putting powder on her nose. He went to her, stood behind her, facing the mirror. She put her makeup down and looked at him.

"*Bellissima,*" he whispered, moving his hand to

her cheek. Her skin was so soft, it was like touching the most precious silk.

"I'm not."

"Yes, you are. You're the most beautiful woman I've ever seen."

She blushed and looked down. "You don't have to say things like that, Nick. It's not necessary."

"Necessary? Of course it is. It would hurt me not to tell you."

"It's not true."

"Only through your eyes." He reached below her chin and gently lifted her face until she'd once again met his gaze in the mirror. "I see a woman whose skin is so soft, I'm almost afraid to touch. Whose eyes are as green and deep as a forest. Whose mouth is so lush, my lips get lost in a kiss."

He let go of her chin, but only so his hands could find her shoulders. Turning her, he felt resistance, but not much. Then she was facing him, and he was looking at the real thing, not a mirror image.

"More than that," he whispered, lightly touching the small lines at the edges of her eyes. "I see your laughter." He brushed the pad of his finger on her brow. "I see the wisdom and the sadness in your eyes." Then he leaned down and gently kissed her lips. "I feel the tenderness, and the passion, and you are so lovely it makes me want to weep."

She moaned, cried out in a sound that was part pain and part surrender. He took her in his arms, and this time his kiss wasn't gentle. He tasted her lips, but it wasn't enough. He slipped inside the wet velvet of her mouth, where the feel of her made him dizzy.

Her hands went to his back, and she pressed herself to him more tightly. Her breasts against his chest made him ache for her, and he reached down between them to touch her.

She jerked back a little, and he stopped. "What's wrong?"

"I'm just a little tender there, that's all."

"Ah," he said, disappointed. "I'm sorry. I got carried away."

"No, really, it's not your fault. *Ormones*," she said, saying the word with his Italian accent. Then she smiled.

He smiled back. It wasn't easy, as he had to concentrate on cooling his body down, but he did it. It wasn't time to press her. She wasn't feeling good, and he wouldn't do that to her. But he knew he would have to make love with her soon. "Feel better?" he asked.

She nodded. "Yes, I'm finished crying. Don't worry."

"I wasn't worried at all."

"Like hell." She reached up and brushed his cheek. "It's a good thing you're a pilot, because you could never make it as an actor."

"You don't think so?"

She shook her head. "But that's okay. I like that I can tell when you're worried about me."

"That's not the only thing I'm thinking about."

"I can tell that, too," she said, her smile broadening. "Only it wasn't the look in your eyes that tipped me off." She moved her hips against him to illustrate her point.

"Do that again, and you'll really see something."

She laughed, and he felt a flush of pride wash over him. Almost strong enough to combat his desire, although not quite. He'd helped her through whatever that was. The tears were gone, and that was because of him.

So, this pregnancy thing wasn't so hard. He thought of Carlo, and all his words of warning. That pregnant women become unpredictable, moody, unfathomable. Clearly Carlo just didn't have the touch. The trick was to listen carefully, that's all. To be patient.

"Let me finish my hair," Jessica said as she turned to face the mirror once more. She picked up the brush. "Where are we going to dinner?"

He moved back to give her room. "I thought we'd go to the Bicycle Shop Café."

She nodded as she pulled the brush through her hair. Nick got caught in the rhythm of her movements. He'd like to do that for her sometime. Feel that soft mane of hair in his hands. There were so many things he wanted to do with Jessica.

"I can't guarantee I'll be able to eat," she said, "but I'll try."

"You still don't feel well, eh?"

She put her brush down. "Nope. I probably won't until the second trimester."

He moved toward her again, and this time he wrapped his arms around her waist so he could rub her stomach. It was still so flat it was hard to believe there was a baby inside. It did feel good, though. Her body pleased him very much. Not so skinny as to be on a magazine cover, but a real woman's figure.

"There you go again," she said, sighing. "Trying to distract me."

He laid his chin on her shoulder while he continued his impromptu massage. "We could call out for food. Get a pizza."

She shuddered. "Oh, no. I don't think I could handle that."

"The pizza? Or staying in?"

She put her hands on his, just as he was moving them down below her belly. "Either."

He frowned.

"Tonight," she added.

He stood up and let her go. "All right. But as soon as you feel better…"

"You'll be the first to know."

"Good."

"I'll get my purse."

He couldn't help but smile as he followed her to the living room. So he didn't get everything he wanted. There was no rush. The important thing was that she had stopped crying. That she felt nice again, cheerful.

"All set," she said, turning off the kitchen light.

He opened the door for her. Then he remembered. "Oh, Jessica, my mother is coming in two days. She couldn't wait to meet her future daughter-in-law."

Jessica stopped, looked at him and burst into tears.

IT HAD BEEN A LONG NIGHT. Jessica had chased Nick out when she couldn't stop crying. He'd protested, but when he finally left, she felt sure he was relieved. She hated this. Hated having her emotions be so rocky. She felt vulnerable, and perhaps that was the worst thing of all. She'd finally fallen into an exhausted sleep, but when she'd woken this morning, she still felt unsettled.

The phone rang, and she knew it was Nick before she picked it up.

"Are you feeling better?"

"Yes, Nick. Thank you. I'm fine."

"Good. Then you can come with me today?"

"To do what?"

"You need to know everything? Maybe I just want to spend some time with you, eh?"

"I don't trust you," she said. "You've got something planned. Something you're afraid to tell me."

He laughed. "Where is the Jessica who climbed the trellis? Who came barefoot into my bedroom?"

"She's clearly back in Rome, because this Jessica isn't going to go outside her door without knowing what you've got on your mind."

She heard him sigh. "Please. For me."

"All right."

"Good. I'll be over in five minutes."

"No, you won't. I have to shower."

"I can help with that, too."

"Fat chance. Give me an hour."

"You drive a hard bargain, Jessica."

"You'd be wise to remember that." She hung up, surprised that she was smiling. Actually looking forward to seeing him. She shouldn't be. Nick was unpredictable. Crazy. He'd invited his mother and sister here, without even asking her. She couldn't imagine what he had in store for her today.

Even so, she hurried to the shower. Instead of the hour she'd requested, it only took her half that time to be ready. With thirty minutes to wait, she picked up her yellow pad. On the first empty sheet, she wrote, Marriage—Pros. Then she began her list.

Unfortunately, it wasn't a long one. But page two, Cons, went on and on. By the time Nick knocked on her door, she was utterly, horribly depressed.

"Something happened?" he asked, the moment she opened the door.

"No," she said. She didn't want a repeat of last night. It took all her strength, but she smiled brightly, forcing herself to forget the list that still lingered in her head. To forget the fact that the only reason he wanted to marry her was because of the baby. That he'd never once talked about love.

"Good," he said. "We have a busy day. First, have you had breakfast?"

She nodded.

"Also good. So we go."

"Let me get my purse." She hurried to her room, checking out her reflection one last time. The sundress was one she liked a lot. Pale green, with soft yellow flowers. She'd worn this once before when she'd been out with Nick. He'd admired it, and since then it had become a favorite.

"Jessica?"

"I'll be right there." She got her lipstick out of her purse and quickly put it on. Then she went out to meet him. He stood at the doorway, leaning casually against the frame. Her heart did that little jig that only seemed to happen around Nick.

He was too good-looking. That should have been her first warning sign. But she was weak. And when he looked at her with those dark brown eyes, she had no willpower. Even now, in his khaki slacks and beige polo shirt, he seemed too beautiful to be real. He was more like something she'd see on the cover of *GQ*. Strong, muscular, regal. It wasn't fair at all that he had the Italian accent, too.

"What's the matter?" he asked, pushing off from his perch at the door. He brought his hand to his face and rubbed his chin. "I didn't forget to shave, did I?"

"No," she said. "Nothing's wrong. I was just looking, that's all."

"At what?"

"You." She stepped out into the hallway. "I thought you wanted to go?"

He shook his head and stepped beside her, closing the door behind him. "I don't understand you," he said. "All you American women. You talk in circles."

"You know us all, eh?"

"I know plenty. And you all are slightly crazy."

"I can't speak for the others, but as for myself…" She stuck her tongue out at him.

He laughed. "You see? Crazy."

She hit the elevator button, amazed that her mood had changed so quickly. Although, with her *ormones,* nothing should surprise her anymore. It was a roller coaster ride. A trip down a blind alley. She never knew what to expect. But as long as her

mood had brightened for the moment, she intended
to enjoy herself.

"HERE WE ARE."

Jessica looked up at the house on the small hill.
It was enormous. A two-story white Tudor mansion. Great old trees lined the driveway, and as they
drove up, she could see immaculate flower beds on
both sides. "Who lives here?"

"Us," he said, parking the car by the door.
"Maybe."

"Nick, you've got to be kidding."

"Why?"

"This is a mansion. It's on Sunset Boulevard. It's
got to be worth millions."

"Yes?"

"Are you really that rich?"

He nodded casually, as if this wasn't a big deal.

"This rich?" she said, pointing to the house.

"My father was a very successful man. I'll tell
you about him sometime. But right now, the real
estate lady is waiting inside."

She couldn't believe it. This wasn't a house she
could live in. Real people didn't live in these man-
sions. Movie stars did. He walked around the car
and opened her door, holding his hand out. She took
it, then climbed out, the house even more awesome
when she stood on the drive.

"Is pretty, no?"

"It's beautiful. But it's huge. A whole city could live here."

"What do you mean? It's only six bedrooms."

"Who's going to use them?"

"You. The baby. And when my mother visits, and Theresa. She'll have children, too. And my cousins, perhaps. Your mother, too. It's important to have enough bedrooms."

She shook her head as he led her to the door. Even that was spectacular. The leaded glass was etched and beautiful, the wood polished to a high sheen.

The woman who answered the door was as elegant as the home she was showing. Taller than Jessica, and slimmer, too, the woman was dressed to the nines in a DKNY suit that Jessica only recognized because she'd seen it on that TV show *Style*. She smiled and introduced herself as Paula Rose, then turned to Nick and doubled the wattage on her grin. Clearly the woman had spent a fortune on orthodontics.

She proceeded to show them the house. Actually, she showed Nick the house while allowing Jessica to tag along. And Nick ate it up. He was charming as hell and made Paula laugh about every two minutes. Oh, the house was gorgeous—the kitchen would have made Julia Child faint from its over-abundance—but it was huge, and Jessica couldn't help feeling like she was in that hotel from *The*

Shining. She'd go crazy here, especially with a toddler.

When they finished the tour, Jessica was not only tired, but cranky. Very cranky. Her stomach wasn't all that stable, and if Nick said one more bon mot she was going to push him down one of the four staircases.

Paula left them alone in the den for a moment, and Nick turned to Jessica with a very pleased smile. "You like it?"

"It's beautiful. But I wouldn't want to live here."

His grin faltered, and that puzzled little-boy expression came over his face. "Why not? It has everything."

"It has too much of everything. I'd get lost here. This is a hotel, not a house." She could see she'd disappointed him. He'd clearly thought she'd be thrilled. But she wasn't about to lie, not about something this expensive. She took his hand in hers. "Nick? It's very lovely, but honestly, it's not me. If I do move, I'd like it to be someplace cozy. Someplace where I can keep an easy eye on the baby. Understand?"

He brought her hand up to his lips and kissed it gently. "Of course. We'll find something cozy for you. I'll tell Paula what you want."

Jessica jerked her hand away. "You will not."

Nick's mouth dropped open.

"I don't like her."

"But, why? She seems a very good real estate lady."

Jessica couldn't tell him the truth. It was embarrassing to admit that she was jealous. "Chalk it up to *ormones,*" she said.

He frowned, then shrugged. "All right. But these *ormones* are very peculiar."

"Get used to it," Jessica mumbled. "I'm a little tired. I think I'll go wait in the car, if that's okay with you."

"Of course. I'll be out in a moment."

It took her about five minutes to walk through the living room and the foyer to get to the door. Once she was outside, she realized she hadn't lied to Nick. She was tired. She got into the car, and that's when it hit her. It wasn't Paula who had upset her. It was her own mistrust of Nick.

Paula was just a sample of all the women whom Nick would charm. Who would flirt with him and laugh at his jokes. It was only a matter of time before the flirting would be too much, and Nick would succumb. After all, he wasn't in love with her. There was no reason to be faithful to her.

Every time Nick went on a trip, Jessica would wonder. What was she thinking? Every time Nick went to the *store,* she'd wonder. What kind of a life was that? Not pretty, that's for sure. Not pretty at all.

Chapter Nine

She was going to be sick. Only this time, it wasn't the baby's fault. This time, it was fear. Nick was due any moment, and with him, his sister Theresa and his mother.

The restaurant was a nice one. Jeff had set it up, and of all the people she knew, he was the best food critic around. It was Italian, of course. Nothing else would do. She was having a little difficulty with the smell of tomato sauce, but that was the least of her worries.

Nick had tried to ease her mind about this meeting, but he didn't understand. It was all still moving too quickly for her. Nick talked as if everything was settled, the marriage, the house, the future. She'd tried to tell him she wasn't sure, but she'd bungled the job. When she was alone, her arguments were calm and rational and terribly clear. But when he came into the picture with his confident grin and that look of paternal glee, she just sort of lost steam.

Now, with his family here, she felt as if she'd lost her chance. Then again, maybe all of this was happening for a reason. Maybe she was just supposed to go along with Nick and get married. The guys certainly thought she should. When she'd suggested to Alan and Jeff that she might back out, they'd looked at her like she was nuts.

They both liked Nick a lot. Hell, everyone loved Nick. As Jeff said, he's gorgeous, loaded and straight. What's not to love?

But did *she* love him? Love him enough to ride this roller coaster all the way through to the end? She'd certainly thought a lot about that one. The problem was, she didn't know the answer. Even if she had, that wouldn't solve the problem. Because she knew he didn't love her.

She picked up her mineral water and took another sip. They should be arriving any second. The waiter kept eyeing the table. Nick was bringing them from the hotel, and the traffic was bound to be bad.

While she was still alone, she reached down for her purse and pulled out her little notepad. It was a new one, devoted entirely to the marriage question. The first five pages were dedicated to Nick. Pros, cons, questions, compromises. With all her writing, with all her attention to detail, she still didn't know what to do.

The pros were very practical. Nick was very

well-off, and would take care of her and the baby quite generously. If they got married, the baby would have a father and a heritage. They'd have a beautiful home, and she was quite sure Nick would be attentive and kind. When he was there, that is.

The cons weren't so concrete. Nick was doing this because she was having his baby. If she hadn't been pregnant, he wouldn't have asked her to marry him. There was no question in her mind that Nick liked her, but was that enough? If she married him, she'd be giving him a great deal of power over her life. Wasn't that dangerous? He was still Nick. He would still travel all over the world, and there was no reason for her to believe that he wouldn't continue to meet women at every stop. Nick had offered marriage, not fidelity.

She heard her name and she looked up. It was Nick. Her hand trembled as she quickly stuffed the notebook back in her purse.

She recognized Theresa immediately. It was the woman from Nick's bedroom, only this time she wasn't wearing a negligee. She was stunning in a red suit so beautiful, Jessica was certain it was couture.

The resemblance between them was marked, and she wondered how she'd missed it the first time she'd seen Theresa. Granted, the situation had been a little stressful, but there was no denying they were brother and sister.

Jessica's gaze moved to the other woman with Nick. Her chest tightened. Surely that couldn't be his mother. God, she'd been so stupid. She'd pictured a stereotypical Italian mother, the kind she'd seen on television. Short, round, in a big black dress, with her white hair pulled back in a bun. Not this elegant woman who looked like she'd just posed for the cover of *Mirabella*.

It was clear where Nick and Theresa got their spectacular good looks. Mrs. Carlucci was stunning. Her hair was dark and thick, worn down around her shoulders like a brunette Veronica Lake. Her figure was perfect, and her dress fit with undeniable grace.

Jessica felt like a country bumpkin. Dreadfully sorry she'd worn her off-the-rack suit and her flats. But Nick hadn't warned her. Damn.

"Jessica," Nick said, holding his arms out to her. "Come, meet Mama."

She stood up, pulling on a smile that she hoped didn't show her panic. Nick took her by the shoulders and kissed her cheeks, then stepped aside, keeping his hand on her arm. "Jessica Needham, this is my mother, Angelina, and my sister, Theresa."

Jessica held out her hand, but then Angelina moved forward to kiss her. Recovering quickly, Jessica moved from cheek to cheek. She got a whiff of Angelina's perfume and recognized it immediately. She'd sprayed the tester at the mall, but it was way out of her price range.

Then Theresa gave her the European greeting. When that was done, Angelina moved forward again and looked her over from head to toe. "Nicky, you didn't do her justice. She's simply lovely."

Jessica realized that she hadn't expected Nick's mother to know English. She'd been wrong about a lot of things. "Thank you," she said.

"I'm sure you don't want to remember me," Theresa said, "but we met once before, eh?"

Jessica nodded. "Oh, I remember."

Theresa leaned forward a little, conspiratorially. "I gave him what for. But good."

Jessica laughed, although it sounded strained. "I'm glad."

"Sit, sit," Nick said, holding out the chair for his mother, then moving quickly behind Jessica. She looked up at him as she sat. He looked so pleased. So happy that his family was here.

He sat next to her and picked up the wine menu. Within two seconds the waiter was by his side, putting down a large basket of bread. Nick ordered a bottle of Chianti, and then brought his attention back to the women. "I haven't had time to tell you, Jessica, but I found a new house. Cozy, just like you want. We'll go see it tomorrow, okay?"

"I understand you work for Main Street Designs," Angelina said. "That's a very good firm. They did Stallone's house, didn't they?"

Jessica nodded. "We do quite a few celebrities' homes."

"That's wonderful. But, I confess, that's not what I want to talk about. I want to hear about you. My new daughter! I'm so pleased to finally be a grandmother."

"You certainly don't look like anyone's idea of a grandmother," Jessica said.

Angelina waved away the compliment, but her smile showed she appreciated it. "I owe that to pasta," she said, then with a sly smile she added, "and a very expensive plastic surgeon."

Jessica was surprised once more. The laughter at the table was easy, friendly and somehow intimate. She tried to imagine her own mother making an admission like that, but she couldn't. Mona would never open herself up like that. Certainly she'd never reveal such a secret.

"The baby..." Theresa said, "Nick says it's due in eight months?"

Jessica nodded. "A little less."

"Oh, I'm so excited! My first niece or nephew. It's all too wonderful. I can't wait. I tell you, we never thought anyone would catch our Nicolo. But now he's going to be a father."

"Have you decided on the name yet?" Angelina asked.

"We're already getting the nursery ready at the villa," Theresa said, turning to Nick. "Just like when we were children. Uncle Bobo found the rocking horse, can you believe it?"

"And the big chest," Angelina added. "The crib is still there, but it needs refinishing."

"We have some time," Nick said.

Just then the waiter came back with the wine, and they all picked up their menus. Jessica couldn't seem to focus. She felt like she was in the middle of a tornado. The conversation leapt from topic to topic, but it seemed she was the only one having trouble keeping up. They ordered quickly and picked up the conversations as if nothing had interrupted them. The waiter stood next to her while she made up her mind. Nothing appealed, so she just asked for spaghetti.

"I talked to Father Lorenzo about the baptism," Angelina said.

"Jessie!"

Jessica turned at the sound of her name. Jeff, Alan and Paul stood two tables away. She shook her head. Wasn't it just like them to show up here? God forbid Jeff should miss a moment. Jessica looked to see if Angelina or Theresa were bothered by the sudden intrusion, but they were all smiles when Nick made the introductions. Before she knew it, the tables were getting rearranged and suddenly the party was in full swing. Jeff seemed completely smitten with Angelina, the way he leaned forward and listened to her. Theresa claimed the attention of Alan and Paul, and Nick just beamed.

She might as well have been a coaster.

"I talked to Father Dillon—" Nick said.

"Father Dillon!" Theresa said, interrupting. "This is a name for a father?"

"He's a good priest," Nick said. "I like him. Anyway, he said we could have the wedding two weeks from Saturday."

"Two weeks," Jeff said. "How the hell are we supposed to get ready in two weeks? That's not even enough time to order the flowers, let alone send the invitations, get a wedding dress, order the food—"

"If we wait, it's going to be another six months," Nick said.

"Okay, in six months, we can do a wedding."

Nick shook his head. "No. I don't think we should wait. We don't have a lot of people coming to the wedding. Just family. Whatever we can do in two weeks, that's it."

"Why?" Alan asked.

"Mama can only stay for two weeks, then she has to go home to help with Theresa's wedding."

"Oh, you're getting married!" Paul said. "Wow, two in a row. That's got to be a pain."

"No, actually, it works out fine," Nick said. "We get married here, then, after the baby comes, we go back to Italy for Theresa's marriage, and at the same time, we have the baptism in a good Roman church.''

The food came, but Jessica barely noticed. She was too stunned. It was as if she didn't exist. As if her opinion didn't matter at all. Nick had found a church? He'd set a date? Rome for a baptism?

''I still say two weeks isn't enough time,'' Jeff said. ''You've got to move to the new house. It's impossible.''

''Did you see that house on Sunset?'' Alan asked.

''If we wait, Jessica will be out to here,'' Nick said. ''Besides, I don't have that much time off. I have to get back to work in three weeks.''

Jeff sighed dramatically. ''It'll be horrendous, but if you insist.''

''We do,'' Nick said, smiling his satisfaction. He turned to Alan. ''Jessica didn't like the house. It was too big. Now, I've found another. Cozy, just like she wants.''

''No,'' Jessica said.

Nick turned to look at her, his expression startled, as if he'd forgotten she was there. The rest of the group quieted, and soon they were all staring. Good. She wanted their attention.

''What's wrong, *cara?*'' Nick asked.

''Nothing. Except I'm not getting married. But you all go on with your plans. I don't want to spoil your fun." With that, she stood up and walked away.

Nick couldn't have been more shocked if Jessica had stood up and sung the National Anthem. Naked.

He looked at his mother and saw the same openmouthed surprise he felt himself. Jeff, Alan and Paul all seemed equally confused. It was only Theresa who wasn't floundering.

"What happened?" he asked.

"I'll explain later," Theresa said. "You go get her. Now."

Nick stood, anxious about leaving his family alone, but not wanting Jessica to get away.

"Go," Theresa said, waving at him. "We can take care of ourselves."

He nodded, then walked quickly through the restaurant, trying to figure out what in the world could have made Jessica bolt like that. And to say she didn't want to get married? It was crazy.

When he got to the parking lot, he ran toward her car, grateful he'd spotted it as he'd come in. Only the car wasn't there any longer. He spun around, searching for her white Honda, and finally he saw her waiting for a big truck to maneuver into a little parking space.

Running full out, he made it to the passenger side and opened her door. Another second, and he was beside her.

"You scared me," she said, holding her hand to her chest.

"I'm sorry. But I couldn't let you go. Please, Jessica, park again. We'll talk, eh?"

She shook her head, then looked straight out the windshield. "I don't want to talk."

"Please, Jessica. I'm confused. I don't understand."

"That's the trouble."

"So if you tell me, I can fix it, no?"

She looked at him, and he saw that she was hurt. Not angry. That only confused him more. What had he done to hurt her? Everything he'd done was for her. "Jessica, please. I want to understand."

She looked like she might cry. He hoped she wouldn't. Fervently. The last time she'd cried, after he'd told her about Mama's visit, he'd felt like a helpless boy. He'd tried to talk to her, to tease her, to make her better, but in the end he'd left her in tears. It had bothered him all that night.

"*Cara*," he said, touching her thigh gently. "Whatever I did, it wasn't meant to hurt you. I hope you believe that."

She sighed, and he saw her shoulders relax. The truck was safely out of the way, and she drove the car a little ways to a more isolated parking spot. Nick didn't speak until she'd put the car in gear and turned off the engine.

"Thank you, *cara*. Now, please. Talk with me."

Jessica turned slightly toward him, but then she looked at her hands instead of him.

"Please?" he whispered.

"It's too fast, Nick. Too much. I can't think straight when it's all rushing at me like this."

"Think straight about what?"

She looked up then, her eyes filled with hurt and confusion. "All of it. The house. The wedding. The baby. You're not giving me a chance. It's all being decided as if I'm just along for the ride. It's my life, too, Nick."

"Of course it's your life," he said. "Your future."

"Then why aren't I being consulted?"

"But I found a new house," he said, trying hard to follow her logic. "It's cozy, only four bedrooms. You'll like it, I know. But if you don't, we'll find another." It didn't make sense to him. They all had her best interests at heart. Everything was about Jessica and the baby.

She shook her head, and he could see the frustration in her face. "That's not the point."

He lifted his shoulders, completely baffled. "I don't know what the point is."

"Nick, you never asked me."

"Asked you what?"

She didn't answer him for a moment, as if she were struggling with something. "You never asked me to marry you," she said finally, her voice so low he barely heard the words.

A great weight lifted from his shoulders, and he fought the urge to laugh. The *ormones,* again. That's what it was. She was upset because he hadn't given her a ring! He should have known.

"Why are you smiling? I don't find this very amusing."

"I know, *cara,* and I'm only smiling because I finally understand. I was a fool. Of course, you're right. Tomorrow, first thing, I'll go buy a ring, okay? Or maybe you come with me? That will be good, because Mama and Theresa can come, too, and then we can all go see the house."

She looked at him as if he were the one with the *ormones.* "Get out," she said.

"What?"

"Get out of my car."

"*What?*" He reeled back, completely off balance. What had he done now?

"Nick Carlucci, if you don't leave right now I'm going to scream."

"But *cara—*"

"Don't call me that." She leaned over his lap and opened his door. "Go on. Get out."

He wanted to stay, but the look on her face scared him. She was going to scream. For what, he had no idea. But for the moment, it was probably best that he do as she asked.

He got out of the car, and before he could even shut the door, she took off. Nick watched the car until she turned the corner two blocks away. The whole time, he kept wondering what in the hell had just happened.

Chapter Ten

Nick went back to the table. Everyone looked up at him, waiting to hear what happened. He sat down, put his napkin back in his lap and shrugged. "She told me to get out."

Theresa shook her head. "What did you expect?"

"What do you mean?"

"You didn't tell her about the church, did you?"

"No, but she'll like it. It's very nice."

Theresa looked at Angelina. "Can you believe it?"

His mother frowned. "No, I can't."

"What?" Nick looked to the men at the table. "What did I do?"

"It's her wedding, Nick," Jeff said. "That's a very big deal in a woman's life."

"So?"

"So she has to be the one to choose."

Theresa took his hand in hers. "Nick, I love you. But you're an idiot."

"Thank you very much."

"You have to listen to her," Theresa said. "Let her decide what she wants."

"But I don't want her to worry about anything."

"There's a difference between choosing and worrying. All the women you've known, and you still don't understand?"

He sighed. "No, I don't."

"Let me tell you something about Jess," Jeff said. "She's one of the strongest women I've ever met. She's logical and practical and smart as hell. She doesn't make snap decisions, and she doesn't like to be rushed. It's just who she is."

"But there isn't time," Nick said.

"Make time," Stan said, scowling at him.

"Listen to her," Alan said.

"Let her make up her own mind," Theresa said.

He looked around the table, clear about one thing. He wasn't doing anything right. What he didn't know was how to fix it. What he knew about women was mostly how to please them in the bedroom. He used to be proud of that. He'd always felt at ease there. Sure of himself, and of what he was doing. Now? He felt like a child. Inept. Confused.

What he wanted was to leave. To get on a plane and fly away. But he couldn't. Not with the baby coming. Not with his mother and sister here.

"Call her tonight," Theresa said, patting his hand. "Tell her you're sorry. That you won't rush her anymore."

"That will do it? That will fix things?"

"I think so," she said. "But mean it, don't just say it."

He nodded. He'd try. But none of this was easy. No wonder he hadn't wanted to get married.

JESSICA WAITED UNTIL the fourth ring to answer the phone. She knew it was Nick. It could only be Nick. Even though she had no idea what to say to him, she picked up the receiver, anyway. "Hello?"

"Please, don't hang up."

"I won't," she said, leaning back on her pillows. She brought her blanket up higher on her chest, then relaxed a little. She glanced at the clock and was surprised to see it was just past eleven. It felt much later.

"Are you still angry with me?"

"Yes," she said. "But not fatally."

"Theresa and I had a long talk," he said. "She told me I was being an idiot."

Jessica laughed. "I like your sister."

"She likes you, too. But she wants to know you better. So do I, Jessica. And I want you to know me, too. Please, let's start again. We'll take it slow, just like you want. No buying houses, no wedding dates. But while Mama and Theresa are here, I'd very much like you to spend some time with them. With us.''

Jessica sighed gratefully. For the first time since Nick had arrived, she felt as though she'd been heard. So it had taken his sister to make him listen. That wasn't so bad. At least he'd finally understood. Perhaps if they did get to know each other better, it wouldn't take an intermediary to explain. ''I'd like that,'' she said. ''I'd like it very much.''

''Really?''

She smiled. He sounded so surprised and relieved that she had to wonder just what Theresa had said to him. ''Yes, really.''

''Good. Then tomorrow, we go out together, okay? You and me and Mama and Theresa. We do whatever you like.''

''Okay.''

There was a long silence where all she heard was his gentle breath. *''Cara?''* he said finally, his voice softer, seductive.

''Yes?''

''I'm ashamed that I hurt you.''

''It's okay, Nick. I know you didn't mean to.''

''It's just that I got excited. About the baby, I mean.''

She winced. Of course it was about the baby. What did she think? That Theresa had somehow made him love her? ''I know,'' she said, struggling to keep the disappointment out of her tone.

"You forgive me?"

"Of course."

"Jessica?"

"Hmm?"

"I could come apologize in person."

She smiled. "Thank you, but it's pretty late."

"You're in bed already?"

"Uh-huh."

"Five minutes I could be there. Maybe four, if I don't hit any lights."

She laughed. "While that's a very sweet offer, I don't think so."

"Sweet? I'm not talking about being sweet, *cara*."

"Really?" she said, only slightly teasing him. "I'd never have guessed."

"Ah, you toy with me."

"I know. I'm a terrible person. Horrible."

"I think I can forgive you," he said, his voice low and sexier than it had a right to be. "But *cara*, it's been too long."

Jessica shifted on the bed, remembering the last time they'd made love. That fateful event that had been such a turning point in their lives. She'd wanted him so badly, so desperately. The truth was, she'd never stopped wanting him that way. But now the stakes were so very much higher.

"Jessica?"

"Hmm."

"What are you thinking?"

"Just that it's late."

"Yes, I see. Well, you get some sleep. I'll call you in the morning, and we'll go to breakfast, yes?"

"Yes," she said. "I'd like that."

"Jessica?"

"Hmm?"

"Lei e cosi bella che quando siamo soli ho para did fare delle pazzie."

"What does that mean?"

"You're so beautiful, I don't trust myself alone with you."

She closed her eyes and took in a deep, steadying breath. "Then we'd better be alone together soon," she whispered. *"Ciao, Nicolo."*

"Ciao carissima."

NICK HUNG UP THE PHONE, then walked over to the sliding glass doors that led to the balcony of his suite. He stepped out into the cool night and let his gaze wander over the brilliant city lights.

He turned toward the east, where Jessica lay in her bed, and wished that he could be with her. Lose himself in her. The irony was not lost on him—she wanted time to think things through, while time to think was the last thing he needed. If he thought about anything at all, it had to be the child. Because thinking about marriage, about being Jessica's husband, scared the hell out of him.

Theresa had explained that he wasn't giving Jessica a chance to choose what she wanted to do, and although he saw her point, he had to wonder what choices were available. Admittedly, he didn't know Jessica as well as he'd like, but he couldn't imagine her not wanting their child to have a father, a name. No matter what arrangement they eventually came to, Nick was determined that his child have every advantage he could give him. Even if she decided that she didn't want to have anything but a paper marriage, that paper was going to mean something.

He'd always appreciated that he'd been born into money, but never so much as when he thought about the things he'd be able to provide for his son. Or daughter. The best nannies, the best schools, the best life possible. The child would be from two countries, which pleased him, and he wanted to make sure that his Italian heritage wasn't lost in the shuffle. He wanted to raise that child equally between Italy and America, and being married to Jessica would make that more likely.

He hadn't realized until tonight that part of his rush to the altar was an attempt to secure Jessica, to bind her to him so that she and the baby couldn't get away. It wasn't very noble of him, but dammit, this was his heir. He couldn't take any chances.

Now he had to slow down, but it didn't mean his

goal had changed. He would convince Jessica to marry him and make sure that his child was raised the way he saw fit. Really, the only thing that had changed was the time it took to get there.

He leaned his arms on the railing and focused on the blinking stoplights far below. He marveled at how his life had changed so drastically in such a short period of time. A few days ago the idea of marriage was the furthest thing from his mind. Now, it was all he thought about. No, that wasn't quite true. He didn't think about the marriage—just the wedding. After that? Well, that was still uncomfortable.

He knew too well what a real marriage took to succeed. Commitment, trust, respect. He had all those things for Jessica, but could she feel those things toward him? Could he ever earn those feelings?

He'd had it good—too good. He was blessed a hundred times with wealth, a fine upbringing, and he had never wasted his looks. He knew full well that women found him attractive—that simple fact had shaped his life up till now. But being handsome wasn't going to help make him a good father. Or husband.

It wasn't all that long ago that his cousin Carlo had told him he didn't have what it took to make a successful marriage. That making it work required sacrifices, and that he wasn't the type.

At the time, Nick had laughed, brushed it off as jealousy. Now he wasn't so sure it was funny. He tried to think of the last time he'd really sacrificed for another person. He couldn't. He'd designed his life to have few obligations. The airlines employed him, but even there he didn't have a full-time schedule. He flew because he liked it, not because he needed the paycheck. His commitment to them was as tenuous as his whims.

As for other people, that was even harder to pin down. He was devoted to his mother and Theresa, that was something that would never change. If they needed him for anything, he would stop the world to be there. But that didn't count. That was family.

He didn't have many friends. Only Carlo and Freddo and Paolo, his cousins. They didn't ask much of him. His lady friends didn't, either. It occurred to him that no one in his life asked much of him. Was it because they didn't have needs, or did they just assume he wouldn't follow through? Did everyone in his life see him as a wastrel? Was that why Jessica didn't want to marry him—because she feared he wouldn't be there for her or the baby? And was she wrong?

This was why he wanted to hurry, dammit. He stood up, walked inside, slammed the door shut. This thinking, what good did it do? Jessica with her charts and lists, all that planning and plotting. All it did was make her crazy, and now she was making him crazy, too.

Well, he wouldn't do it. He wouldn't think these thoughts, that's all. His job now was to convince Jessica that he would be a good father. That's all. The rest...well, he'd deal with the rest when it became necessary.

Chapter Eleven

Breakfast was to be in Venice.

As Jessica drove into the parking lot at Venice Beach, she wondered if Angelina and Theresa had ever been to this mecca of aging hippies, body-builders, in-line skaters and sidewalk merchants. If not, they were in for a treat.

She loved coming here, to walk on the long, winding path that skirted the ocean, to watch the people and marvel at how crazy Los Angelinos really were. She hoped the guy who juggled jigsaws would be there. That was something they'd have to see to believe.

She found a good spot and pulled her car in, then locked it and headed for the restaurant. This meal would surely be more successful than dinner had been last night. She doubted Nick would push her, not with Theresa on her side. Her goal was to get to know his family a bit, to see what kind of relatives they were going to make for the baby. Even if she didn't marry Nick, Angelina was going to be her child's grandmother. It struck her that no matter what, her life was now and forever entwined with this man's. Nothing would change that. Not love, not marriage, not anything. Unless, of course, they chose to close her and the baby out.

She thought about Mona and the tenuous connection they had. Her mother had never been terribly demonstrative, had never really participated in her life, except where she'd had to. And when Jessica went to college, Mona had moved on to Colorado to lead the life she'd wanted, instead of the life she'd been obligated to.

Who was to say Nick's family wouldn't do the same thing? Politely yet firmly inform her that while the baby was to be included in their lives, she wasn't necessary?

That thought chilled her, and she had to struggle to smile when she saw Nick outside the restaurant, waving her over.

"Come," he said, "we have a table."

She met him at the door, and he leaned down to kiss her cheek. The small gesture felt intimate yet familiar, as if they'd greeted each other this way a hundred times. Then she felt his arm circle her waist, and he led her through the airy dining room to a table in the back.

She was struck again at how lovely Nick's mother was. Dressed in a pale yellow silk T-shirt and slacks, she looked cool, comfortable and elegant all at the same time. She could imagine Angelina on the Riviera, sipping champagne on her yacht.

Jessica wished she'd worn something else. She'd chosen leggings and a cotton tunic, simple, easy to wear and plain as white toast.

Theresa also looked gorgeous in a blue sundress, her long dark hair held back with a matching scarf. God, what was she doing with these people? They were Europe and sophistication, and she was L.A. and Target specials.

But Angelina held her arms out, and Jessica walked into the fold. This time, Angelina didn't give air kisses. This time she gave a hug, a real one. A genuine smile. A welcome.

"I'm so glad you're here," Angelina said.

Theresa waited for her mother to let go, then she moved to Jessica to give her own embrace. "I'm just glad you didn't let my brother run you off. I tell you, he's more trouble than he's worth."

"Hey," Nick said, smiling broadly. "I'm worth twice the trouble."

Theresa shook her head and gave Jessica a conspiratorial wink. "Good thing he's not an egotist, eh?"

Jessica nodded. "Right." She hugged her once more as she whispered, "Thank you for last night."

"It was nothing. He would have figured it out eventually. I just gave him a shortcut."

Nick held Jessica's seat for her, and then did the same for Angelina. Once they were all settled, Jessica watched the interplay between the three of them as she pretended to look at the menu.

Nick touched his sister's arm, then her hand. She smiled at him with such affection that Jessica couldn't help but feel jealous. She'd longed for a sister her whole life. Was it possible that she was finally going to have one?

Even if she did marry Nick, there was no guarantee that she would be welcomed into this family, and she'd better remember that. They were all on their best behavior now. But how happy could they really be, having this American nobody suddenly turn up pregnant? She would wager there were any number of Italian women who were going to be mighty upset when they discovered that Nick was off the market.

But Angelina and Theresa were certainly not going to let on that they were disappointed in her. Not yet, at least.

"Jessica?"

She turned to Nick, getting the feeling that he'd been trying to talk to her for a while. "Yes?"

He jerked his head toward the waiter who was standing by her side.

"Oh, I'm sorry. Just some tea and toast, please."

"That's all?" Angelina said. "That's no breakfast. You're eating for two now, darling."

Jessica really wasn't hungry, and nothing appealed. But she didn't want to cause a fuss. "Okay," she said to the waiter. "Two scrambled eggs, well done, please."

The waiter nodded and then left. They must have all ordered before her. She couldn't hide behind the menu any longer, and she found that she was nervous. More nervous, for some reason, than last night. Perhaps she'd had too much time to contemplate who she was with, and what this was all about.

"So, Jessica," Angelina said, "tell us about your family. Nick has told us nothing."

"That's not his fault," she said. "I haven't told him much."

"You're from Los Angeles?" Theresa asked.

Jessica nodded. "Yes. My parents were both born here. I didn't know my father, so I can't tell you much about his background, but my mother's family originally came from Ireland. They came to the States about three generations ago. My grandparents were the first to settle on the West Coast, though."

"And your mother, she's here with you?"

"No. She lives in Colorado."

"She must have been so thrilled when she heard the good news!" Angelina said.

Jessica debated her answer. If she told them

Mona's real response, they'd be shocked, she knew that. But did she want to start this whole relationship with a lie? "Actually, my mother and I aren't very close," she said. "We only speak a couple of times a year. When I told her about the baby, she wasn't particularly interested."

Angelina looked at Nick with such shock that Jessica wished she had lied. She wanted to explain that it wasn't her fault, that Mona was just Mona, and not like other people. But she held her tongue. Better Nick's family understood from the get-go that she didn't come from a warm, fuzzy home, that Mona was more like a distant cousin than a June Cleaver mom.

"I don't understand," Angelina said. "She wasn't interested?"

Jessica shook her head. "My mother is a little unusual," she said. "She's never felt very bound by family ties."

Angelina gave Nick a look Jessica didn't understand—sharp, almost angry. Then she turned to Jessica with a warm smile. "We are very bound to family ties," she said. "And now you're part of our family."

Jessica's hand went to her stomach. "Thank you," she said. "I know that you'll all care very much for the baby."

"The baby? Of course, but the mother, too."

Jessica held her breath for a second. How she

longed to believe that. When her gaze turned to Nick, she saw that he was looking at her with that same sort of confused affection as his mother. As if he didn't quite understand who he'd gotten himself involved with.

"You didn't tell me," Nick said.

"What?"

"About your mother."

She shook her head. "It didn't seem very important."

"I don't understand, Jessica. She can't possibly be as disinterested as you say. You're her daughter. This is her grandchild."

"You don't know Mona. Don't look so glum. It's not a tragedy."

"Yes, I think it is."

She smiled, appreciating his concern, yet feeling embarrassed, too. "Thanks. But I have Jeff and the guys at work. They're like family. They certainly butt in like family."

"Jeff, he's the tall one?" Theresa asked.

"That's right. He's like a brother to me. We've known each other for years and years."

"Well, that's something," Angelina said, although she didn't seem pleased. "Ah, the food. I'm starving."

Jessica's gaze went back to Nick as the waiter served. He still looked upset. She reached over and took his hand in hers. "Please don't worry about it," she said. "It's not a problem."

"You should have told me, Jessica."

"Why? That wouldn't have changed anything."

"Maybe I could have helped."

"That's sweet, Nick, but there's nothing you can do to change my mother."

He shook his head as if there was only a limited amount of clue in the world, and she hadn't gotten her share. "I could have helped you, *cara*. You wouldn't have had to deal with her alone."

That stopped her. Doing it alone was the only way she knew. There hadn't been anyone, ever, to lean on. Oh, she had Jeff and Stan and to some degree Alan and Paul, but she never had shared the really tough stuff with them. Not until after she'd figured out what to do. They all supported her, and cared about her, but when it came down to brass tacks, she'd always flown solo. She wasn't even sure she could share like that. It wasn't something she'd thought about since she was a young girl.

Back then, she'd wished for a sister or brother, someone who could help her along the way, but when that dream died, so did the idea of asking for help. Mona always told her she'd have to live with the consequences of her actions, so she'd better be damn sure she made her choices for herself.

Even now, with this momentous decision before her, it had never occurred to her to ask anyone for help. If she married Nick, it would be because she'd weighed the pros and cons and concluded that marriage was the best possible course. That system had worked very well, and she saw no reason to change things now.

Not that she didn't like the idea of having someone to confide in, to share her fears and her hopes with, but she also knew that was a sentimental notion. When it came to the really hard choices, there wasn't room for sentimentality. She'd learned that the hard way.

"What are you thinking?" Nick asked.

She realized she'd been staring at him for a long while. "Nothing," she said. "Just daydreaming."

"Your eggs are getting cold."

She turned to her plate. Her stomach rebelled, however, and she quickly averted her gaze. She grabbed a piece of dry toast and nibbled on it, willing the morning sickness away.

"Tell me about Nick," she said, turning to Angelina. "What was he like as a boy?"

Angelina smiled. "Ah, now, there's a topic."

"Wait a minute," Nick said. "I'm not sure I like this."

"It's too late, Nicolo," Theresa said. "We're going to tell her all your secrets."

"No, not that! Not all of them. I still want her to like me after breakfast."

Angelina laughed. "Don't worry, darling, I

won't tell her everything. Yet.'' She winked at Jessica. "But I will tell you what he did at Christmastime when he was ten.''

Nick groaned. Jessica leaned forward, anxious to hear all about him as a boy. He must have been so beautiful. He probably got away with murder because of it.

"Nick was always encouraged to work to earn money, even from the time he was a boy. If he wanted something, he had to figure out a way to pay for it on his own.'' Angelina sipped her coffee, keeping her gaze on Jessica over the rim. "The Christmas when he was ten, he wanted to buy some very expensive things, and even though he worked for his father, running errands, doing chores, he clearly didn't feel that it was the most efficient way to earn his money.''

Nick shook his head. "I have no idea what she's talking about,'' he said. "I was a perfect child.''

Theresa burst out laughing. "Perfect? You were a little monster!''

"Only to you, because you were such a *marmocchio*.''

"What's that?''

Theresa laughed. "He means I was a brat.''

Jessica laughed. "Go on,'' she said. "Don't stop now.''

"On Christmas Eve morning, we were awakened by a loud knock on the door. It was very early, maybe four o'clock. Nick's father and I got out of bed, scared to death. Who should be on the steps? Nicolo and two policemen!''

"What did he do?''

"He went swimming." Angelina laughed. "He was soaking wet, shivering, without shoes.''

"It seemed like a good idea at the time," Nick said, unable to keep the smile from his lips, although Jessica could see he was trying. "I only did it because I wanted to buy you a present.''

"What?" Jessica asked, although she had an idea. "Where was he swimming?''

"The Trevi Fountain is where," Angelina said. "He'd gotten up in the middle of the night and taken a pillowcase with him. He climbed down from his window. He didn't even take a coat, and it was very, very cold. The police found him stuffing the coins into the pillowcase. He'd nearly cleared out the whole fountain!''

"No." She looked at Nick and shook her head. "You really thought you could get away with that?''

Nick, his face tinged with pink, sat up very straight. "It was perfectly legitimate. I made a wish, and it would have come true, if not for the police.''

"What, you wished for all the money in the fountain?''

"That's right. I just decided to help it along a bit.''

Jessica couldn't keep from laughing. She could picture it all so easily. How angry he must have been to have his plan thwarted.

"He was furious," Theresa said. "Outraged. The police didn't arrest him, but only because Papa talked them out of it. And they made him pay, didn't they, Nicolo?"

"They were unfair. Horrible."

"Not so horrible," Angelina said. "He had to go every night for a month and help clear the coins from the fountain, and then count all the money."

"They worked me like a slave," he said.

"Poor guy," Jessica said. "It must have been hell."

"I had a cold, too. But they didn't care."

"You were sick because you went into the fountain in the middle of winter!" Angelina said. "What did you expect?"

"I expected it to work."

Jessica leaned back, listening to the laughter of this family. There was such joy, such affection in the sound, that it made her throat tighten. To be a part of this, to be one of them, would really be something. Maybe it was too late for her to learn to share, but it wouldn't be for her child. No matter what happened, she wanted her baby to know this sound. To feel this warmth, this intimacy. And maybe, if she were very lucky, she could feel like she belonged, too.

JESSICA TRIED HARD not to listen to Nick's phone call. The unexpected rush of emotions had come from nowhere and had caught her completely off guard. What she didn't understand was why she was feeling this way at all.

Maybe it was just because she was tired from all the sightseeing, or edgy from being with Nick's family. There really wasn't a logical explanation. After all, she'd known Nick was a pilot from the first day. She'd liked the fact that he was well traveled. She knew he loved his job, and that he would continue to fly until he was too old to sit in the cockpit. None of this was news. So why was she feeling this way, just because he was planning his next flight?

She wiped her eyes with the back of her hand as she filled her teakettle with water. This pregnancy was making her nuts. Of course it was just her hormones going crazy. Why else would she be so emotional? It wasn't as if she'd expected Nick to change jobs just because she was going to have a baby. For heaven's sake, lots of pilots had children, and they all seemed to get along fine.

But if she hadn't expected him to quit, why did she feel so betrayed?

She put the kettle on the stove and turned on the burner. Maybe she hadn't expected it—but she had hoped. Somewhere in the recesses of her hormone-riddled brain, she'd hoped that Nick would realize that his job would take him away from her and the baby, and that he wouldn't want that to happen. Right. Was she nuts? It wasn't sensible. It wasn't fair. It wasn't logical. Yep, she must be nuts.

Knowing she was crazy didn't seem to help. She still felt like hell, and she couldn't stop herself from imagining all sorts of horrible things. Nick in Paris, meeting a French beauty. Nick in New York, meeting an American beauty. Nick meeting all the beautiful women in the world. Nick giving in. Nick falling in love with someone else.

She hugged herself as she waited for the water to boil. This wasn't good. This was awful. If she was this upset before he left the ground, how was she going to live through an actual flight?

Damn, she'd never thought of herself as a jealous person. But she wanted to scratch the eyes out of every female who even looked at him. Stewardesses! God, she hadn't even thought of them. They would stay at the same hotels. Bring him coffee in the cockpit. Flirt. Tease. Cajole. How could they help it? He was the best-looking man in two countries, for heaven's sake. He was everything a woman could want, and he had the added allure of being Italian. They wouldn't care that he had a wife and baby at home. They would stop at nothing until they had him in their clutches.

Damn, damn, damn. She flung open the cupboard door and grabbed two mugs. She nearly ripped the silverware drawer out, then banged it shut so hard the glasses shook. She turned to the stove and cursed at the kettle.

"What's this?"

She swung around at the sound of Nick's voice.

"Did I really hear those words coming out of your mouth?" he said as he approached. "I'm shocked."

"Don't be. I have plenty more where that came from."

"Well, I can't say that I blame you. Imagine, having the temerity to be so slow to boil. I think you're absolutely right to curse out the water."

"You're making fun of me."

"Yes, I am."

"I wouldn't do that if I were you."

"Why not?" He came very close to her as she leaned against the counter. Very close. Only inches away. "It's something I enjoy. And I think I'm good at it, no?"

"Oh, so it's a sport with you, is it?"

He nodded, his gaze holding her captive. "It's right up there with soccer as my favorite pastime."

"Really? Do you know what I do to people who make fun of me?"

"I'm insulted that you include me with anyone else."

"Oh, I've been made fun of by the best."

"Nonsense. They can't hold a candle to me."

"Arrogant bastard."

"Ah, there's that language again. Call me something else. It makes me crazy for you."

"No."

"You sadist."

She nodded. "You have no idea."

He moved another inch closer, and she felt his warm breath on her mouth. "Show me," he whispered. And then his lips were on hers.

Chapter Twelve

How had he waited so long to do this? Nick moved his arms around Jessica's body and brought her closer as he deepened the kiss. Tasting her set off wildfires in his body, leaving him no choice but to seek relief. He felt her breasts against his chest and the intoxicating sweet curves of her hips and stomach.

She teased his tongue, licked his lips, moaned softly, and that was all it took to make him hard and aching. Moving his hand to her breast, he cupped her, feeling her stiff nipple beneath her shirt.

She pulled back with a little yelp and he froze.

"I hurt you?"

"It's just that my breasts are tender."

"I won't touch—"

"No, it's all right. As long as you're gentle."

He met her gaze, searching for reassurance. She nodded, then took his hand and placed it once more on the soft mound of her breast. He sighed, then kissed her again.

The teakettle burst into a whistle, and once more Nick stepped back. Jessica reached over and turned off the stove. When she faced him again, he could see his own hunger echoed in her eyes. "Come with me," she said, taking his hand.

She led him past the living room into her bedroom. He'd not been here before, he realized. He'd only seen the front of her apartment. The last time they'd made love, they were in his hotel room. He liked this better.

Her bed looked inviting with the fluffy white comforter and pillows. But he paid little attention to his surroundings. The woman in front of him was too compelling, and his need for her too strong.

God, she was beautiful. More beautiful than when he'd first met her. Was it their baby that made her skin so luminous? That made her eyes shine like that? He reached over and touched her hair, soft, silky, shining. he let his fingers linger for a moment, then slowly moved them down to her face.

Jessica closed her eyes, and he touched her as if he could see through his fingertips. He wanted to memorize every nuance, every inch. Her cheeks, her lips, her brows. All of them felt impossibly perfect.

Now he needed to see more. He moved his hands down to the hem of her top. She opened her eyes, and he hesitated. Was that doubt he saw there? "I can stop now," he said, surprised at how gruff his voice sounded, and how hard it would be to keep his word.

"No," she said. "I want this. I want you."

Hearing her declaration made him feel strong, somehow. He wasn't sure why, only that it was true. The need to protect her felt like a physical part of him, like his skin or a rib. He knew then that no matter what, he was going to do everything in his power to keep her safe.

He lifted the hem slowly, his gaze breaking away from hers just as the material cleared her breasts. She raised her arms, and he pulled the top the rest of the way off. The bra she wore was lacy, pink, demure. He could make out the darker skin of her nipples, and he remembered seeing her naked for the first time. How he'd been amazed that her body was so lovely and soft. She didn't have any sharp edges, which seemed a remarkable thing for a person. Every place he touched welcomed his hand or his lips. It wasn't that Jessica was so different from other women, but his reaction to her was unlike anything he'd experienced before. Looking at her now, so sweetly vulnerable in that slip of material, he wondered if she felt it. If making love with him perplexed her. He didn't dare ask. What if she said no?

Instead, he moved his hand, very gently, to the

top of her breast. He let his fingers trace the edge of the lace.

"Nick?"

He tore his gaze from her flesh to her face. "Yes?"

"Tell me something?"

"Anything."

"If I wasn't... If I wasn't pregnant, would you... No, never mind."

"What? Would I be here tonight?"

She nodded.

"It may not have been tonight, but I would have been here."

"Why?"

"What do you mean?"

She placed her hand above his, holding it firmly above her heart. He could feel the steady beat, the very life of her. "I mean, what made you come back here? What did you hope would happen?"

He studied her eyes, humbled as always at the trust he saw there. She expected the truth from him, no fancy words, no embellishment. But what was the truth? "I hoped that we could start again," he said finally. "That I could convince you somehow that my invitation was sincere."

"Then what?"

"I can't answer that. Can you?"

She gave him a funny little smile. "Probably not.

But I can tell you what I wish would have happened.''

"What?"

"This."

It was what he wanted to hear, but he had an idea it wasn't all she wanted to say. He thought about pressing her, encouraging her to tell him all that was swimming in that fertile mind of hers, but his body…his need was so very real and her skin was so very soft.

When she brought her hand behind his neck and pulled him down to her lips, any intention he might have had fled like smoke in a storm.

Jessica let go. She let go of her worries, her questions, her doubts. What she was going to do with Nick didn't need explanations. It was something she'd wanted for a long time. Since Rome. When she was in his arms, she was safe. And right now, she needed that haven. A mindless, endless fall into deep waters where she could happily drown.

She let her hands have their way, exploring and touching without hesitance. His chest, so firm and hard, and then down to his flat stomach. She felt him take a breath as she went lower still. He moaned as her fingers played along the length of him, and felt again how firm and hard he was.

He broke the kiss, but only so he could play delicate games with her earlobe, and then his lips were on the soft hollow of her neck. It was her turn to moan when he dipped lower, tasting and licking the skin just above the top of her bra.

She felt the clasp of her bra open, and his fingers moved in tandem to her straps, pulling them down her shoulders. She let her hands fall to her sides, and the bra fluttered to the ground.

He touched the very tips of her nipples with the palms of his hands. It wasn't even a touch, but a whisper that teased her into twin erections. It was exquisite torture not to lean into those palms, but she held herself completely still. He moved his hands in slow circles, never really touching her, yet igniting her nerve endings to a nearly impossible pitch.

Finally, she gave in and moved an inch forward. His hands, still gentle, cupped her fully and she sighed.

"Is this okay?" he asked, his voice soft and concerned.

She nodded, closing her eyes. "Oh, yes."

Then she felt his lips replace his right hand. Soft, warm, wet, she trembled at this new maneuver. She'd never been this sensitive, and the more he ministered to her, the more anxious she became to have him inside her.

She touched the back of his head, then reached down to his shirt. He got the picture immediately and stood up to undress. Jessica watched his chest as it was bared, impressed again at the beauty of his body. Lightly muscled, firm and tan, his chest had a smattering of dark hair. She remembered the feel of his hair, and how she'd been content to lie in his arms and let her fingers play there. She also remembered how his dark curls tapered off to a narrow V.

Nick undid his pants, and that spurred her to remove her own. With a quick tug, she was undressed, stepping away from the last of her clothes.

Nick looked at her, from her toes all the way up to her face, and he didn't hurry. She was surprised that she wasn't self-conscious, but it was clear he took pleasure in seeing her. Although she knew it wasn't possible that she was showing already, she put her hand on her stomach. Nick smiled and put his hand next to hers. "It's hard to believe."

"I know," she said. "But in a few months it won't be."

He rubbed her tummy and kissed her. "I want to see every change, *cara*. I want to watch our child grow in you."

She kissed him back, moving so her body and his touched from chest to knee. "You won't mind when I'm all big and swollen?"

His smile answered first. "I can't imagine anything more beautiful than to see you heavy with child."

"Well, damn," she said. "You keep saying

things like that, and I'm going to be forced to do something drastic.''

''Oh? Is that supposed to scare me?''

She nodded. ''Uh-huh.''

''Do your worst,'' he said. ''Just remember that my memory is long and revenge is sweet.''

''Are you saying that whatever I do to you, you'll do back to me?''

He nodded, giving her a smile that was half devilment, half desire.

She brought her hand down and encircled him. He took a sharp breath, and his eyes closed. Now that she had him where she wanted him, she wasn't about to let him go. Slowly, with a patience she had to struggle for, she rubbed his length, feeling his heat and his need in the palm of her hand.

Without opening his eyes, he followed through on his promise. She felt his hand on her stomach, sliding down, teasing her flesh with the lightness of his touch. When he reached the juncture of her thighs, it was her turn to close her eyes. She found herself shifting position, spreading her legs to give him access, but never letting go of him or changing her pace.

When he moved his finger inside her, she felt him harden further. She wasn't going to be able to take this for long. The torment was too sweet, and she was afraid her knees would buckle. But damn, it felt so wonderful. Nick was a magician, touching her in a way designed to drive her insane.

"Oh, *carissima*. What you do to me."

"You're not too shabby yourself."

"Come with me."

"Keep touching me there and I will."

He laughed, but then he moved his hand away. Taking her by the arm, he walked her to the bed. Not bothering to bring down the comforter, he climbed with her onto the bed until they were nestled together in the middle, facing each other. His hand wandered over her side, then to her back. As he reached her behind, he pulled her tighter to him, and she wallowed for a moment in the closeness. Then he was kissing her, and all the patient slow moves were gone, replaced by an urgency that arced between them like flames.

No more thinking. Only feeling. Only being swept away in a tidal wave of heat and sweat and sensations and the utter acceptance that when he was inside her, she was whole.

HE WOKE UP AT ONE in the morning. He tried to remember when they'd crawled under the covers, but he couldn't. Everything after that second time was a blur.

She was sleeping, curled up next to him with her hand flung over his chest. Nick turned until he could comfortably watch her, deciding his glass of water could wait. Her hair, wild from all that movement and sweat, was somehow more beautiful for its abandon. Normally, Jessica kept her hair combed, and it was good to see this side of her. He'd known from the first that she was a wild one, even in her proper suit with her proper pearl earrings. The duality of her intrigued him in a way he didn't understand, but he thought it might have something to do with the fact that she fooled so many people. She even fooled herself. But not with him. Not in bed.

He breathed deeply, filling himself with her scent. The sweetest perfume in the world. Unique, earthy, it couldn't be bottled, nor would he want it to be.

Sighing quietly, he brushed her cheek with the back of his hand. What in the world had he gotten himself into? How was he going to make her happy for a lifetime? It was a job for a better man than he. She needed someone stable, someone with both feet on the ground. He could give her material comfort, at least he had that to offer. But happiness? Security?

The phone call this evening from the airlines had set him thinking. If he continued with his international flights, it would mean spending a great deal of time away from Jessica and the baby. He'd not be able to take much time off, if he wanted to continue to work for a major company. He supposed he could find out about doing local runs from Los Angeles. That would keep him home a great deal more. But a milk run from L.A.? That wasn't flying. That was taking off and landing, over and over again.

He'd become a pilot for the adventure. For the opportunity to see the world and meet the women. But how fair was that to Jessica? She'd be unhappy with him, and he couldn't blame her. It wasn't a career for a married man. Not the way he liked to fly.

Who was he trying to kid? He was nothing if not selfish. Everyone in his life had made sure he knew that. He hadn't felt particularly badly about the fact before now. But looking down at that face of hers, he finally understood that being selfish was not a virtue.

Nick got up as quietly as he could. Before he left the bedroom, he made sure Jessica was still asleep. Her even breathing told him he hadn't awakened her. He slipped on his boxers and made his way out of her room.

Once he was in the kitchen, he turned on the light. He grabbed a glass and poured himself some water, then he sat down at her table.

Looking around her living room, he saw things he hadn't noticed before. Plants, for one. Why hadn't he known she liked plants so much? He counted four without getting out of his chair. And then there was that picture on the wall. A Rothko print. She liked modern art. He didn't know the first thing about modern art.

The truth was, he was about to marry a stranger. What he did know about her, he liked a great deal. Too much, perhaps. He had no desire to disappoint Jessica. Yet, it was inevitable. Modern art wasn't the only thing he didn't know the first thing about. Being a husband, a father. Both of those jobs felt helplessly out of his league. What he was good at was the short term. Wooing a woman. Moving on. Making a good first impression. None of those attributes would do him much good as a papa.

An image of his own father came to him. Before he'd become ill. He'd idolized the man. Worshipped him. At least for his business sense.

His father had been a tremendous success in business, a good father, but not a good husband. Mostly he hadn't been there. When he was, he'd made Angelina unhappy. Why did his mother love him so much, when he'd been such a scoundrel? And Theresa, she also loved him. Why? Why?

"What are you doing?"

He jerked his head toward Jessica's voice. She was standing in the hallway, dressed in a long silk kimono. Looking so delicious he could barely stand it. He held up his water glass. "Thirsty. Can I get you one?"

"I think I'm up for that tea I never had." She

walked toward him, the kimono opening so that he got a glimpse of her thigh. Unbelievably, he felt himself harden again. He hadn't been stimulated so much in one night since his early twenties.

"It's late. Won't tea keep you up?"

"Not this kind. It's chamomile. No caffeine."

As she passed him, she ran her hand over his back. The light touch made his situation worse.

"You don't happen to have any food in that refrigerator, do you?"

Jessica turned the stove on, then went to the fridge. "In the mood for something substantial, or something wicked?"

"I don't need wicked from the kitchen, when I've had so much in the bedroom."

She laughed. "Well, that's where men and women are different. Because I always want something wicked in the kitchen."

"Is that an invitation?"

"No, that's carrot cake." She pulled the dessert out and brought it to the table. "Can you stand it? It's the only thing I've been able to eat without getting sick."

"Better that than pickles and ice cream."

"I suppose," she said, sitting next to him. "But I really can't understand why I couldn't crave something good for me. Like salad or cottage cheese."

"What fun would that be? Isn't having a baby all about eating for two?"

"I suppose. Only I'm the one who's going to have to live with my body after the baby is on its own."

He reached over and put his hand on hers. "I like a big woman," he said. "None of this skeleton chic for me."

"Now I'm really depressed."

"Why? What did I say now?"

She pushed the cake away. Stared at it with disgust. Then pulled it back. "Just get me a fork and shut up."

He laughed as he obliged her, glad he knew where she kept her silverware. He sat again, watching her eat. It fascinated him, the way she almost made love to the confection. No simple cut, bite and swallow for his girl. No, each piece had to have a perfect ratio of frosting to cake. Each and every bite was accompanied by a sound. He recognized that sound from about two hours ago. It signified great pleasure, although he wasn't at all sure he shouldn't be upset that she was enjoying carrot cake as much as she had making love to him. But he was from Rome, so he understood the great communion between food and people.

She hardly looked at him while she ate, and when the teakettle whistled, he prepared her tea. Finally, she finished, and from the look on her face, he might have guessed that he'd witnessed another climax.

"That was worth every ounce," she said.

"You certainly do have a healthy appetite," he said, "and not just for food."

She smiled a little guiltily. "I'm just enthusiastic, that's all."

"Yes, I know."

"What were you thinking before?" she asked, her demeanor changing abruptly. "When I came in, you looked worried."

"Me, no. What would I have to worry about?"

"The fact that your entire life is about to change, perhaps?"

"Oh, that."

"Yeah. So you want to talk about it?"

He thought about lying to her, but that was only his pride speaking. "I am worried," he said.

"Oh." Jessica's gaze went from his eyes down to the table.

"Not about you," he said, reaching his hand over to hers. "About me."

"What do you mean?"

"I've never been a father before. It's worrisome."

Her gaze moved back up. "I've never been a mother, either."

"You? You'll be perfect. Of all the people in the world I'd want to have my child, you're the one."

Again, her gaze skittered away. Evidently he'd said the wrong thing. "Jessica?"

"Hmm?" She stood up to put the cake back in the refrigerator.

"I mean it. I'm not just saying words. I really can't imagine a better mother."

"Thank you, Nick. I know you mean it, and I appreciate it."

But something was still wrong. She wouldn't look at him. He stood and moved over to where she was leaning against the counter. He captured her hand, and when that wasn't enough, he reached under her chin and lifted her face until she met his gaze. "What is it, *cara?* What did I say that made you unhappy?"

"Nothing."

"You must be forgetting who you're talking to. You can't lie to me, Jessica. I'll always know if you are."

She sighed. "I really do appreciate what you said. It's just that..."

"Yes?"

"God, it sounds so selfish."

He chuckled. "That's something I understand, too."

"It's just that through all of this, you've never once said you loved me."

"I...I..."

She broke free from his grasp and ran out of the kitchen. He stood there, knowing he'd just hurt someone he cared about very much. But did he love her?

Chapter Thirteen

Jessica sat on the edge of the bathtub and pulled her kimono tightly around her. All she wanted was for Nick to leave. What made it worse was that it was her own damn fault. If she hadn't asked the question, he wouldn't have given her his answer. Knowing for sure that he didn't love her was infinitely worse than pretending he did. She should have just kept her mouth shut.

All her illusions about her future came crashing in—that this child was born of love, that Nick would have married her, anyway, that they had a chance in hell of being happy. It seemed ludicrous that she'd even had those thoughts. They were all based on some idealistic notions she should have abandoned years ago. Funny thing, but for once in her life she agreed with Mona. Love was a fantasy, a fairy tale. It was a panacea for the weak.

His knock on the door made her jump.

"Jessica?"

She didn't want to talk to him. Not when she was feeling this vulnerable. God, when they'd made love she could have sworn… But that was a fairy tale, too. Not on her part, unfortunately. The tragedy of this was that she loved him. She didn't want to, but that didn't seem to matter much. She had fallen in love with Nick about ten minutes after they'd met. And now look at her.

He was going to marry her, but only because of the child. Why not? What did he have to lose? He would still have his life; hell, he'd barely be around. She was the one who'd be stuck in a loveless marriage, with all the time in the world to have her regrets.

"Jessica, please. Let me in. Let me explain."

"There's nothing to explain, Nick."

"I didn't mean to hurt you."

"I know. Don't worry about it. I'm fine."

"If you were fine, you'd be out here."

"I just want to take a bath."

"Open the door, Jessica. Please."

She couldn't avoid him forever, even though that's what she wanted. It took all her strength to stand, to walk to the door and open it.

"Thank you," he said softly.

"For what?"

"For giving me a chance to make amends."

"There's no need. Honestly."

"But there is. We're in a strange circumstance, Jessica. And we need to talk about it."

She couldn't look at him. If she did, she was going to cry, and that was simply not acceptable. "It's late. Can't we talk about it tomorrow?"

"No. Now. Come with me," he said, reaching for her hand.

She moved away. "I can't do this now. I don't feel well."

"Jessica, I do love you."

Her head snapped up. "Don't. Don't go there. I'm warning you, Nick, if you start lying to me I'll never forgive you."

"It's not a lie."

"Bull. You're only saying you love me so I'll go through with the wedding. Well, I have a news flash for you. I'm not going to marry you. I won't deny you access to the baby, but dammit, I'm not walking into a marriage that's based on nothing. I won't do that."

"*Cara*—"

"Don't call me that!"

"Jessica, please. I was stupid, that's all. I do love you, you have to believe me."

She studied his eyes. She tried to find the lie there, but all she saw was concern. If he loved her, though, he would have said so when she asked. This was all too little, too late. "I really want to take my bath now."

"Don't. Don't close this door, Jessica."

"I have to."

"No, you don't. You can come and sit with me. Talk with me. Don't dismiss me because I was caught off guard. It's not fair."

"Fair? Since when does fairness have anything to do with it?"

"All right. I'll grant you that. Let's look at it logically, then. It doesn't make sense for us to ignore this. You're the one who's always talking about looking at issues from all angles. That's all I'm asking for. Give me a chance to show you the angles."

"What angles could there be? You either love me or you don't. There's no half way."

"No? You're an expert on love, are you? You know all the ways a person can be in love?"

"I suppose you might love me the way you love a hot fudge sundae, but frankly, that doesn't cut it."

"You're impossible. These *ormones* of yours make you think like a...like a..."

"Female?"

"Exactly."

"Well, pardon my lack of a y chromosome."

"Mi stai facendo impazzire!"

"I have no idea what you just said, but I resent it."

Nick threw his hands up in the air and said something else in Italian. She meant to go past him, march into her bedroom and lock the door. But he kept waving his hands around, pointing at her, then up at the sky, then back at her again. All with the accompaniment of what she could tell were old Roman curses.

She was just about to teach him some good old American curses when she noticed his boxers. Mickey Mouse? He was wearing Mickey Mouse underwear? She burst into laughter.

He stopped talking to look at her. It was clear he thought she was ready for the men in the white coats, but she couldn't stop. It hurt, she was laughing so hard. She held her side and wiped her eyes. Finally, she pointed to his drawers.

He looked down. And she watched him turn red, starting with his chest then moving slowly up his neck to his face. That made her crack up harder. She had to sit. She plopped down on the toilet seat and wrapped her arms around her aching stomach.

"These were a gift," Nick said.

"Oh, yeah. Right," she said, struggling to stop laughing.

"My mother brought them for me. My cousins went to EuroDisney."

"Okay," she said. "I believe you."

His blush got deeper, and he wouldn't look at her. She could tell he wanted to run away, but then he'd never run from her. Not just because she'd caught him with his pants down. But because he was too much of a man.

"I thought you'd like them," he said. "But I guess I was wrong."

"No, no. You aren't wrong. I love that you wore them here. For me. They're darling."

"That wasn't exactly the reaction I was hoping for."

"Oh, Nick. What am I going to do with you?"

He smiled as he walked over to sit on the side of the tub. "I don't know," he said. "But I hope you'll stick around to figure it out."

She'd lost all her outrage. Not her fears. They were still there, as real as ever. But it was impossible to stay angry at a man in Mickey Mouse underwear.

"Do we have a deal?" he asked, taking her hand in his.

"I'm not going anywhere."

"Good." He stood. "Now, come back to bed with me. We'll talk."

"I know you mean that in the most generous sense, and I don't want you to misinterpret what I'm going to say, but can we talk tomorrow? I'm so tired I can't see straight."

"Of course," he said, pulling her to her feet. "We can talk tomorrow, and the day after that. I'm not going anywhere, either."

She looked at him sharply. "I thought you had a flight scheduled."

"Not for another week. I didn't want to leave while Mama and Theresa were here."

"I see," she said. But she didn't. She let him walk her back to the bedroom, and she crawled under the comforter. He snuggled next to her, wrapping his arm and leg around her so she was cocooned in his embrace. She was grateful that her back was to him. This way, he wouldn't know she was crying.

JESSICA TOOK A LAST LOOK at herself in the tiny mirror of her compact. No mascara under her eyes, no shine on her nose, no lipstick on her teeth. She closed the compact, put it in her purse, then stood up straight. It was going to be fine, she was sure of it. Angelina and Theresa had invited her over so they could get to know each other better. Not to scare her away from Nick.

But her heart still pounded as she knocked on the hotel room door. She'd barely lowered her hand when the door swung open. Theresa beckoned her in, her smile wide and generous. "Come in," she said in that charming accent. "We've been so anxious for you to get here."

"Thanks." Jessica was once again treated to a warm hug. She'd been prepared, and yet it was still hard for her to relax in the embrace. Probably because she'd had so little experience with physical affection in her own family. Jeff and Paul were both very affectionate, and hugged and kissed her often, but that wasn't the same thing.

Theresa took her hand and led her into the living room. The suite was stunning and astonishingly large. Much bigger than her apartment. It was always a shock to remember how wealthy Nick and his family were. Although they all dressed to the nines, they weren't ostentatious. But man, this was some room!

The paintings on the wall were all impressive and, she was certain, originals. The baby grand by the window was a Steinway, for heaven's sake. Jeff would have had an orgasm looking at the furniture. It was opulent yet comfortable. Elegant without being obnoxious.

"Sit," Theresa said. "What can I get you to drink? We have Evian, fruit juice, tea, soda?"

"Orange juice would be wonderful."

"Perfect," Theresa said. "Not to make you jealous, but we were thinking a mimosa before dinner would be divine."

"Don't worry about it," Jessica said, sitting on a burgundy mohair club chair that was as cozy as it was striking. "How was your day?"

Theresa left the well-stocked wet bar with their drinks. She put Jessica's down, then went to the nearest couch and made herself comfy. It was all

Jessica could do not to laugh. Here she'd taken such pains to look her best—silk pants and matching blouse, pearl earrings, high heels—and Theresa was in a pair of jeans with a Donald Duck T-shirt. Probably a gift from the same cousin.

"Hello, darling!"

Jessica turned at Angelina's greeting. She stood up, and Nick's mother rushed over to give her a hug. It felt so warm that Jessica was ashamed of her uncharitable thoughts.

"So good of you to come tonight. We've been wanting to spend time with you away from everyone. We're very selfish, my daughter and I. We don't like to share."

Jessica laughed. "I'm all yours."

"Good." Angelina looked at her glass. "I see you've got your drink, so sit. I'll just get one for myself, and we'll talk, yes?"

Jessica nodded. As she sat back down, she watched Angelina. The woman was so impressive. There was an innate sense of style about her, a grace and charm that Jessica had only seen a few times in her life. It came from breeding, she thought. From being trained in etiquette and social graces from birth.

She'd like her daughter or son to have that. Just like Theresa and Nick, she'd like her child to be socially adept, charming, at ease anywhere. She'd also like her child to be comfortable hugging and touching like Nick's family was.

Angelina came back and sat next to Theresa. Looking at the two of them, she couldn't help but think that if this had to happen, it was really quite wonderful that it happened with Nick. It would have been infinitely nicer if he loved her, but she'd learn to deal with that. There were so many pluses for the child, that she felt selfish and petty, wanting it all.

"Nick tells me that you like lists," Angelina said.

Jessica had to smile. "It's not so much that I like lists, as I find them a useful tool."

"What do you mean? Tell me about these lists."

"They're nothing, really. If I'm faced with a dilemma, I write down the pros and cons of each choice. It helps to clarify things."

"Do you always choose the one with the most pros?"

Jessica nodded. "Sure. Why do it if I'm not going to use the information?"

Angelina's brow furrowed. "But what about your..." She turned to Theresa and they spoke rapid Italian, then Angelina faced Jessica once more. "Your guts. Is that right?"

"Yes, that's right. I'm not very comfortable going with my guts. I don't trust them very much."

"No? I can understand if you want to buy a car,

you make a list. But if the question deals with your heart?''

"Ah, those are the most important questions." She sipped her juice.

"Mama, I think Jessica is very smart. She knows that emotional decisions are sometimes wrong. This way, she stops and thinks about things. *Si?*"

"That's the idea, at least."

"All right," Angelina said, "then let's make a list of the pros and cons of you moving to Rome."

Jessica nearly dropped her glass. "Pardon?"

Theresa glared at her mother for an instant, then turned a brilliant smile toward Jessica. "What Mama was trying to say is that we were wondering if you'd given any thought to the idea of moving to Rome."

"Quite frankly, no, I haven't. Is that what Nick wants?"

"We haven't talked to him about it yet. First, we wanted to see if it was something you'd consider."

Angelina nodded. "This is my first grandchild. I would like so much to watch him grow up. It's hard to think of being so far apart."

"And we could help, too," Theresa said. "When you want to go out, we could watch him."

"My nephews both have little ones, so the baby would have playmates," Angelina said.

"The nursery at the villa is so beautiful."

"You could stay home with the baby."

"We could have so much fun!"

"The child would grow up with family all around."

"Wait!" Jessica held up her hand to stop the barrage. "I get the picture," she said. "And I'll certainly consider moving to Rome as one of my options."

"Don't forget," Angelina said, "Nicolo will be flying so much. You'll be alone here."

"We just want what's best for you and the baby," Theresa said. "But don't misunderstand. You don't have to. We just wanted to make sure you knew that coming to live with us was, as you say, an option."

"Thank you," Jessica said. Her head swam with this huge new chunk of information. She'd never once imagined that Nick's family would want to participate so much in the raising of her baby. It was an idea so foreign to her, she barely knew how to feel about it. On the one hand, it scared her. She'd be a stranger in Rome, amid all of Nick's family. She didn't even speak Italian! On the other hand, the idea of the baby growing up in a big family was something she'd never dared hope. It seemed too outlandish to want something as wonderful as that.

"We've scared her, Mama."

"No, Theresa, you haven't. You've just given me a lot to think about."

"So we must go eat," Angelina said. "No one can think properly on an empty stomach."

Jessica laughed. "How can you stay so slim, with an attitude like that?"

Angelina sighed. "Simple. I don't think properly."

Theresa stood up and held out her hand to Jessica. "Don't believe that for a moment. She's a very smart woman."

"You don't have to convince me of that," Jessica said, taking her hand. She stood up, but Theresa didn't let her go.

The phone rang, and Angelina went to answer. When she was out of the room, Theresa looked at Jessica shyly. "I'd love you to be my sister," she said. "I always wanted one, you know."

"Me, too," Jessica said.

"Nick's waiting downstairs," Angelina said as she came back from the bedroom. "He wants to know if he can join us."

Both women looked at Jessica. "I don't see why not," she said, hoping she wasn't committing some kind of faux pas.

"Good," Angelina said. "Because I already told him it was okay."

"Mama!"

"What?"

"You don't know Jessica well enough to do that."

"But now I know her better," she said, taking her purse from the counter, "and she knows me better, too."

Jessica smiled. She knew both of them better after this talk. What she didn't know was what to do. She followed Theresa and Angelina out to the elevator, but she really didn't pay attention to what they were saying. There was too much to think about.

It would be very scary, moving to Rome. She wasn't sure that was the right answer for her, or for the baby. But to deny the baby all the love this family wanted to shower him with would be cruel, wouldn't it? Hadn't she always dreamed of having a family like this for herself?

It would mean marrying Nick, of course. Even though she knew he didn't love her. But as far as she could tell, that was really the only drawback. Everything else about the marriage was on the plus side. And there was a chance that if they did marry, Nick would eventually come to love her.

She couldn't count on that. She'd better not. That was dangerous thinking. If there was one thing she prided herself on, it was her logic. And logic said that she'd better accept Nick for what and who he was, and never, ever expect him to change.

The elevator stopped, and Jessica followed Theresa and Angelina to the restaurant. Nick was waiting at a table, and he stood up as they approached.

He barely looked at his mother or sister. His incredible smile was just for her.

"*Ciao, cara,*" he said, stepping to her side. "I hope they haven't said too many bad things about me."

"We wouldn't," Theresa said. "Nicolo, you know better than that."

"He only says those things because he knows it shocks you," Angelina said.

"Well, it's not nice."

Nick laughed as he held Jessica's chair for her. When she sat, he leaned down and kissed her on the neck. His warm breath made her shiver in a completely delicious way. Then he whispered "I missed you" before he stood up again.

She didn't say a thing. She just watched as he went to his mother's side and kissed her cheek, then did the same to his sister. Her gaze stayed on the women. It was so clear they adored him. She already knew he adored them.

"So," Nick said as he picked up his menu. "Did they convince you to marry me? Or scare you away forever?"

"Yes," she said.

He laughed. "Yes, they scared you?"

She shook her head.

His smile faded. "They convinced you to marry me?" he said, his voice a little unsteady. He glanced at his mother and sister, but they both gave him shrugs instead of answers.

Jessica took a deep breath. She felt as if she were jumping off a high cliff, and she couldn't see what was below. But this was for her baby. She smiled, then nodded.

"*Cara,* are you sure?"

"Yes."

He didn't say anything for a long while. He just stared at her. Looking for what, she didn't know. But he must have seen it, because he gave a little nod, grinned like a Cheshire cat, grabbed his water glass and stood up.

"Mama, Theresa," he said. "I thank you both for doing what I couldn't. Jessica has agreed to be my wife."

Both women jumped up and came to her side. They were so happy, so enthusiastic, that she felt— no, knew—she'd made the right choice. For the baby.

Angelina kissed her cheek. "I couldn't be happier, darling. Unless, of course, you decide to move to Rome."

"What's this?" Nick asked, looking sharply at his mother.

"We thought it would be lovely, Nicolo. Jessica and the baby in Rome, at the villa. Don't you think so?"

Nick was so slow to nod, that Jessica almost took back her yes. If he didn't want her there...

"Of course, it's a grand idea," he said finally. But she didn't quite trust his smile.

"Good." Angelina stood up and turned to Nick. "When are you going to make an honest woman of her?"

"Saturday."

"What?" Jessica asked, afraid she'd heard him correctly.

"I never canceled the church," he said. "We'll be husband and wife in six days."

"To the wedding," Angelina said, lifting her glass.

"To the wedding," Theresa and Nick echoed.

Jessica lifted her water glass, but couldn't quite say the words.

Chapter Fourteen

Nick sipped his wine as Angelina, Theresa and Jessica talked about the wedding. The more they talked, the stronger the urge to run out of the restaurant became. Not that this wasn't what he wanted. No, he'd asked her to marry him, and he still believed it was the right thing to do. But ever since he'd made love with Jessica, this marriage had become a lot more complicated than he'd anticipated.

Before, it had just been what he had to do. No self-respecting man would do less. It was his child, and he would see to it that the boy had every advantage, including the Carlucci name and birthright. It had been a nice bonus that the mother of his child was someone he liked. Liked well enough for him to have followed her to America.

Now it wasn't just about the baby. It was about Jessica, too. He knew she had expectations of him as a husband. What he didn't know was what those expectations were.

Did she want him to be a full-time husband and father? Did she expect him to change diapers? Or would she be content to have the comfortable surroundings he could provide, without him?

Even more perplexing was the fact that *he* didn't know what he wanted. Was it possible to have his old way of life without hurting her? He didn't think so.

"Nicolo," Theresa said, "tell her."

"Tell her what?"

"Haven't you been listening?" Angelina asked. "We've been talking about the villa. About Jessica and the baby moving to Rome."

"What?" He looked from his mother to his sister and, finally, to Jessica. Her eyes told him he'd messed up again. But they'd sprung this on him with no warning!

"Don't worry," Jessica said, "I'm not moving."

"Please, darling," Angelina said. "Don't say that. You promised to think about it, didn't you?"

Jessica nodded, but when he tried to capture her gaze, she wouldn't look at him.

"I think it's a wonderful idea," he said, although he wasn't at all sure he was telling the truth. "But only if it's something Jessica wants."

"Of course," Theresa said. "But it wouldn't hurt if you helped her want it."

"No need to rush things," Jessica said. "I think getting married in six days will provide us with enough panic to last a while."

"And there's the house to buy."

"Nicky," Theresa said, "if Jessica comes to Rome, you won't need to buy a house."

"Whether she moves or not, I want her to have a home here. She'll visit back and forth, no? And I want her to be comfortable."

"All right," Theresa said hesitantly. "But don't make it too wonderful."

"I know a shop where we can get your gown," Angelina said. "We'll have to go tomorrow if we have any hopes of getting something decent."

"Of course we need to talk to Jeff about the wedding party," Theresa added. "He said he couldn't do anything in less than a month."

"He'll change his mind for Jessica." Nick's mother turned to him. "When we finish shopping for her, perhaps we can get you fitted for a new tuxedo?"

Nick nodded. A tuxedo was the least of his problems. He had some serious thinking to do, and there was no possibility he could do it in the midst of all these wedding preparations.

He watched the women in his life for a moment. Angelina and Theresa were thrilled, that was clear. But when his gaze moved to Jessica, he could see all his own doubts and fears on her face. Why had she changed her mind?

JESSICA STARED AT HER reflection in the mirror. This was it. The one. The dress she would be married in.

Behind her, Angelina and Jeff argued over a veil, while Theresa and Paul eyed the dress she was wearing critically, speaking to each other as if she were a mannequin.

"I'm not sure," Paul said.

"But look what it does for her bosom," Theresa argued. "The line is perfect."

"There's absolutely no train. And look at those rosettes on the sleeve. What's that all about?"

"This is it," Jessica said.

"Let's try on that Vera Wang one more time," Jeff said.

"And maybe the Jessica McLintock," Angelina said, holding up two veils for inspection.

"If we can stop thinking white, white, white," Paul said, "we wouldn't have to worry about her hair."

"This is the one," Jessica said again. She turned to her entourage. "I want this dress."

Everyone finally heard her. They studied her from head to toe, not one of them looking very pleased.

"It'll work," Jeff said, as if his pronouncement

made the decision final. "With her hair back, dropped pearls and loads of baby's breath in the bouquet."

"What about the veil?" Angelina asked. "I think this one, no?"

The attention shifted to Angelina, and Jessica sighed. She appreciated the fact that her friends and her future in-laws had all wanted to come with her to select her dress, but she also felt an emptiness in the pit of her stomach.

Her own mother should have been here. Well, not her mother, but the mother she should have had. Instead, she had to borrow friends and family. They were all wonderful, but it wasn't like in the books. On the other hand, what about this wedding had been ideal? She still wasn't sure she was making the right decision. It was as far as the baby went—that's why she was here now. The baby came first. But a wedding was supposed to be the happiest time of a woman's life, not a compromise.

That's what her wedding was, though. A compromise. One or two more pros than cons. A slight tilt of the scales. And she was picking out veils and silver patterns.

The week was going by so quickly, she barely had time to catch her breath. The entire design team had put everything else on hold and had pulled together a wedding party that she still could hardly believe. After the ceremony at the church, they would all go to the Mondrian Hotel, where there would be a sit-down dinner for forty people. Almost all of them friends of the groom. She was stunned that so many of his relatives were coming from Italy. Everyone from his grandmother to his second cousin Luigi.

On her side, it was mostly business associates, some of her friends from college, and her aunt Ruth, who was flying in from Delaware. Jessica had no idea if her mother was going to show up or not. She'd called to invite her, but Mona wasn't sure she could get away.

"Hey, you doing okay?"

Jessica jumped a bit at the sound of Jeff's voice. He had come up next to her, and she hadn't even noticed. "I'm fine, thanks."

"How come I don't believe that?"

"Oh, Jeff. You know I'm a natural-born worrier."

"That's not what I'm concerned about."

She looked in the mirror again and ran her hands down the gown. "Do you like it?"

"Don't change the subject." Jeff walked in front of her, blocking her image. "Talk to me, Jess."

"There's nothing to talk about."

"Then why won't you look at me?"

She forced her gaze up, willing herself not to show the confusion that was swirling inside her.

But that, it seemed, was too big of an acting challenge for her.

"Honey, tell me what's going on?"

"It's just that this isn't what I thought it was going to be like."

"The dress?"

She shook her head.

"The wedding?"

She nodded, feeling her eyes fill with hot tears.

Jeff moved in and wrapped his arms around her. She laid her head on his chest, grateful that he wasn't going to see her cry.

"Don't you love him?" he said.

"That's the problem. I do love him. If I didn't, all of this would be a lot easier."

"So you're marrying him because of the baby?"

She nodded.

"You know, you don't have to. You won't be alone, kid, ever. You've got me and you always will. No matter what."

The tears she'd been fighting spilled over. She tried to speak, but she couldn't.

"For what it's worth, I think he's a good guy," Jeff said, his voice so low she had to struggle to hear him. "I don't know if that makes any difference. But I like him, and his family. I think you could do a lot worse."

She sniffed and wiped her cheek. "I'm just being

a sentimental fool, that's all. Nick is a nice guy. He'll be a good father, that much I'm sure about.''

"He could end up being a good husband, too, you know. Stranger things have happened."

"Yeah. I know. I'm just…"

"You just want it all, right?"

She nodded again, knowing she was wetting his shirtfront with her tears.

"You deserve it all, sweet one. You don't have to do this if you don't want to. Just follow your heart."

"My heart is what's gotten me into trouble."

She felt more than heard him laugh. "Isn't that always the way?" he said. "But hey, at least you're in good company. I don't know anyone who hasn't made a damn fool of themselves for love."

"I'd rather not join that club if it's all the same to you."

"Too late. Seems to me you're a card-carrying member, and have been ever since you got on that plane to Rome."

She sighed, wiped her eyes once more and stepped out of Jeff's embrace. She looked up at him, at his wry smile. "Thank you for being here."

"It's my job," he said, winking.

She smiled. "I think I have to go try on some veils."

Jeff leaned down, kissed her on the cheek and

put his hand on her stomach. "That's one lucky kid
you got there."

She put her hand over his. "He sure does have
a remarkable uncle."

"TO THE HAPPY COUPLE!"

Nick smiled as he heard the clinking of glasses
all around him. He turned to Jessica and held out
his own glass. "To the happy couple," he said
softly. She smiled and brought her water glass to
meet his.

Having finished his toast, Jeff sat down, and
everyone began to eat. The rehearsal had gone well,
and the reward was this dinner, a preview of what
they could expect after the wedding. It looked wonderful, but Nick found he wasn't particularly hungry. He hadn't been for the last several days. According to his mother, it was nerves, and he
believed that. With so much to do in so little time,
he was bound to be edgy.

Just this afternoon he'd put a bid on the new
house, the cozy one that Jessica had finally ap-
proved of. It was in Santa Monica, and it was very
nice, if a bit small. There were four bedrooms, at
least, and a swimming pool. What did it matter, as
long as Jessica was happy?

He'd also had his last tuxedo fitting and helped
Jessica pick out china and silver patterns. No one
had told him getting married was such a compli-

cated affair. He'd be glad when all this was over, and he could go back to the calm of the cockpit. But he only had to wait one more day. By this time tomorrow, he'd be married.

He shifted his gaze to his bride-to-be. She wasn't eating, either. That wasn't good. She had the baby to think about. "Jessica?"

She looked up. "Hmm?"

"If you don't like the salad, I'm sure they could bring you something else."

"Oh, no, I like it fine."

"Really?"

She nodded, giving him a wan smile.

"Are you all right, *cara*?"

"Of course. Just a little tired, that's all."

He could understand that. She'd been swept up in all the preparations. Now that he really looked at her, he could see that she was exhausted. She was pale, thinner than she should be. "Tomorrow, you can sleep late, no? We don't have to be at the church until one."

She laughed. "Tomorrow I'll be at the beauty shop bright and early."

"Do you have to? You look so pretty now, what do they need to do?"

"Now, that's sweet. Wrong, but sweet."

"I wasn't trying to be sweet. You need to rest."

"I'll rest the day after tomorrow," she said.

"We can postpone the honeymoon," he said. "It's not too late."

"No, I think a few days in Palm Springs will be wonderful. Please don't worry. I'm fine."

"You don't look fine. You look tired."

She patted his hand. The touch surprised him, and judging from the expression on her face, it surprised her, too. It occurred to him that they hadn't touched in days. They hadn't been alone, they hadn't really talked, they certainly hadn't made love.

His gaze moved from their hands to her face. She was staring at him, as if he were a stranger.

"That's funny," she said.

"What?"

"Nothing. It's silly."

"Tell me."

She smiled, the first genuine smile he'd seen in a long while. "I was just thinking about the first time you held my hand."

Instantly, the moment came back to him. That first night, when they'd left the party and gone for a walk on the beach. He'd taken her hand, and something had happened. A jolt had gone through him. An almost electrical spark. He'd felt it again, just now. "I remember," he said.

"You felt it?"

He nodded. "Then, and now."

She didn't say anything for a minute. She just

looked at him, her gaze unwavering and deep. "I'm glad," she whispered.

He leaned over and kissed her gently on the lips. Feeling her again, tasting her, he felt a surge of relief wash through him, although he wasn't sure what he was relieved about. "I've missed you," he said.

"I'm glad about that, too."

"What are you doing tonight?" he whispered. "After?"

She shook her head. "Nothing."

"Would you like some company?"

She nodded. "I think that would be very nice."

He smiled. "It's a date." Then he turned back to his meal and realized he was very, very hungry.

BY THE TIME HE'D DROPPED off his family and made it back to Jessica's apartment, it was after one. He almost knocked, then remembered the key she'd given him three days before. When he got inside, it was dark, except for a light coming from her room. He hurried toward her, anxious to touch her again, to make love. It had been impossible to think of anything else since the salad course.

He went into her room, and there she was. Lying in bed, sound asleep. He thought about waking her, but he couldn't. She needed her rest. But God, how beautiful she was. How he wanted her.

Instead, he left her there and went back into the

living room. He flipped on the light and started to undress. The question now was should he shower or just go to sleep? He walked over to the kitchen table and put his shirt on the back of a chair. Then he just stood there, listening.

It was very quiet. He heard the hum of the refrigerator, but that was all. It wasn't a sound he was looking for after all, he realized. It was the peace. The feeling of being home.

He turned off the light and went back to the bedroom. Staring at the dark form under the covers, he shed his pants, shoes and socks. Then he lifted up the comforter and crawled in next to Jessica, taking great pains not to wake her.

She shifted once, and he froze, keeping himself still until he was sure she was still asleep. Then he moved close to her, cupping his body against her so that he felt her from his chest to his toes. He slipped his arm around her waist, and rested his cheek on her hair.

Breathing deeply, he wallowed in her scent. She smelled of flowers and powder, and it was perhaps the nicest scent in the whole world. Her heat flowed from her body to his, and he sighed.

For once in his life, he was where he belonged. Holding her like this, he finally understood that instead of a trick of fate, Jessica's pregnancy was a gift from a guardian angel.

He still didn't know if he could be the kind of

husband she deserved, but he knew he was going to try. He didn't understand this incredible need to protect her. To keep their child safe. But it over-whelmed him, blocking out everything except…

It hit him, and it hit him hard. He loved her. He loved Jessica. The earth didn't shake, the heavens didn't roar. Nothing changed, except that he let go of all the nonsense he'd been clinging to for so long. He wasn't being trapped. Far from it. He was being rescued. This is where he wanted to be. Lying next to this woman. Feeling her soft skin, breathing her scent, basking in her warmth.

Someone was watching out for him. He felt sure of it. On his own, he wouldn't have had the courage to marry Jessica. But now that he was here, that it was all coming to pass, he was grateful.

He closed his eyes, feeling more relaxed than he ever had in his life. He'd tell her, in the morning. First thing.

Chapter Fifteen

Her side of the bed was empty. Nick realized it before he even opened his eyes. When he did, he found her note on the pillow. She'd gone to the beauty shop, and he wouldn't see her again until she walked down the aisle. She'd signed the note with just her name. Not "Love, Jessica." Just "Jessica."

He looked over at her clock. It was almost ten; he'd overslept. Launching himself out of bed, he hurriedly put on his pants, socks and shoes, then went to the kitchen to retrieve his shirt.

Grabbing it quickly, he knocked a yellow pad from the chair seat. He bent down, glancing at the words on the page. Another one of Jessica's lists. But this one made him pause. This one was about him.

He probably shouldn't read it. It was personal, private, but he couldn't help it. Not with a heading like Marrying Nick.

He felt quite heartened at the fact that the page had only pros. First on the list was that he would be a good father. She went on to list his family, security, wealth, health, even the fact that he had accepted her gay friends without batting an eye. Funny that she would think about that. When he reached the bottom of the page, he realized it wasn't complete. He turned to page two, and there he saw what he'd dreaded. The cons.

Nick looked away. Perhaps he would be better off not knowing what she didn't like about him. But how could he change if he didn't read them? No, he should put it down right now and get out of here. He had to get to the hotel, shower, dress and make sure his family and friends all made it to the church by one.

His gaze moved to the page. Just a quick look, and he'd leave.

The first thing he saw made him regret his decision. Jessica had written down that even though marrying Nick was the right decision for the baby, she wasn't sure it was the right decision for her.

Second on the list was his job. He'd be away so much, that she would have almost no help from him on a daily basis. Number three was that she would never be sure he wasn't meeting some other woman on his travels.

His face heated as he realized all his private fears hadn't been so private, after all. He should have known that Jessica was bright enough to figure out his dilemmas and make them her own. He couldn't blame her. He had debated seeing other women while he was on the road. How was she to know that he'd abandoned the idea?

He hadn't even known it until last night. But it was true. He knew it so deeply, there was no argument, no loopholes.

He had to sit down. Pulling the chair out, he managed it, but unsteadily, like a drunk. Not because of her list. But because he realized that his decision to honor their vows was not out of duty or honor, but out of love.

Not the kind of love he was used to. This was a whole new experience for him. His need to protect her wasn't just for the baby's sake. The baby didn't have much to do with this feeling. It was a nice bonus, but if something happened tomorrow, if they found out she hadn't been pregnant after all, he'd still be glad they were married.

Steadying himself, he looked back at the list. It wasn't much better. He made decisions without consulting her. He rarely touched her, unless they were making love. He never asked her about her work, or what she planned to do about it after the wedding. *He didn't love her.*

That one got him. He sat down and flipped back to the first page. Every one of her reasons for marrying him had to do with the child—not him. Not them.

It was entirely his fault. But he could fix that. He would fix that. He'd tell Jessica how much he loved her. That she could trust him. That he wanted this marriage with all his heart.

As he rose, he buttoned his shirt, then fished his keys from his pocket. He was determined to make this a wonderful day for his bride.

THE STYLIST WAS PUTTING the final touches on Jessica's hair, the makeup artist was waiting for her turn, while the manicurist applied the last coat of quick-dry on her nails. She was being pampered and cooed over by everyone in the shop.

In the station to her right sat her future mother-in-law. To her left, Theresa. Two other Italian relatives were across the way. Everyone was drinking mimosa cocktails.

It should have been the most exciting morning of her life. Yet all she could think about was the fact that she was walking into a world of heartache. She hadn't changed her mind. She wouldn't. This was for her baby, and there was no sacrifice too great where her child was concerned. She just wished with all her heart that she didn't love Nick. Then this whole thing would be so much easier. More like a business arrangement than a real marriage. It was loving him that doomed her, and she knew it.

"Jessica? Are you all right?"

She turned to Angelina and smiled. Determined not to let her misgivings spoil the day for anyone, she nodded. "Just a little overwhelmed, I think."

"Of course. But don't forget to enjoy yourself, darling. This is your special day. Except for the birth of my children, my happiest memory is my wedding day. How excited I was! How nervous. I'd only known Nick's father for a short time, you know."

"I didn't. I'd like to hear about it."

Angelina smiled and closed her eyes. The stylist took out the last of her curlers, and began brushing her hair. After a quick sip of her orange-juice-and-champagne cocktail, Angelina sighed. "I met him at the Trevi," she said. "You visited the fountain?"

"Yes," Jessica said, remembering that morning, and her wish. It certainly hadn't come true. She was indeed a fool for love. And she supposed she always would be.

"I was nineteen. Young and full of dreams. He was a student, and in a terrible hurry, carrying an armload of books across the piazza. He ran into me, boom, and all the books flew out all around. His papers started to fly into the air, and we rushed to catch them before they were lost or fell into the water. We got almost all of them, but three hit the fountain. Marcello didn't hesitate a moment. He went into the water in his shoes and his pants, to get his papers. I thought to myself, what a foolish young man. Surely a few papers didn't matter so much. But when he came back to apologize to me, he explained that the papers weren't his. They belonged to a friend. He could do nothing less than go after them, even if it meant ruining his one good pair of shoes.''

Jessica could picture it easily. Angelina must have been gorgeous at nineteen. Marcello never stood a chance. He was probably smitten from that moment on.

"He was so handsome. Like Nicolo. A beautiful boy. And, I confess, I was quite pretty back then, myself.''

"You still are," Jessica said.

"Bless you, darling. But when I was a girl... Anyway, he asked me if I would go with him to a dance that evening. I said yes. I think it was while we danced under the stars that we fell in love. It was only a matter of telling my parents, and his, and waiting for the church that stopped us from marrying that very night.''

"Oh, how romantic," Jessica said. "It sounds wonderful.''

"It was. Even though we were poor back then, we were happy. We had our moments, don't mistake that. He had a passion for his business that sometimes made me feel lonely, but for the most part, we were so good together. And how he loved his children!" Angelina looked at Jessica. "Nicolo will be like that, you know. A wonderful father."

"I know," Jessica said. "There's never been a question in my mind."

"He'll be a good husband, too, darling. Trust me. He's like his papa. They have their flings from time to time, but that's men, eh? Marcello always came back to me, and Nick will always come back to you."

Jessica didn't know what to say. Her mother-in-law was telling her that her husband would have affairs, but that it didn't matter. That her own husband had betrayed her, and she didn't care. Maybe it was because Angelina was European. Maybe in Italy, infidelity was no big deal. But Jessica was from Los Angeles, and for her, it was a very major deal.

It was up to her, of course, to change. To shift her attitude so that when it happened to her, she'd be more like Angelina. If she was going to survive it, she'd have to change. Nick wasn't going to. Why should he? He'd be away so much, and in his culture it wasn't frowned upon.

She looked at Angelina again and realized she'd said something else about her husband. Jessica scrambled for something to say that wouldn't expose her feelings. "How long has he been gone?"

she asked, hoping her voice didn't sound as shaky as she felt.

"Three years in July," Angelina said. "And I miss him every day."

"I'm sorry."

"Don't be. I'm not. We had the best life imaginable. No regrets."

Jessica sipped her orange juice. Would she be able to look back at her marriage to Nick with no regrets? She doubted it. She thought about yesterday's conversation with her mother. Mona had called to say she couldn't make it to the wedding. That she had other plans. Although it was expected, it had still hit Jessica like a physical blow. No matter how much she tried to convince herself that she didn't want or need her mother's love, it was no good. Every rejection was like the first. Every disappointment put another arrow in her heart.

Now, here she was, getting married to a man who didn't love her. Asking for the same grief. For the same heartache. At least she understood the way it worked. There would be no surprises. And she'd have the baby.

NICK ARRIVED EARLY. He wanted to catch Jessica as soon as he could, but she wasn't at the church yet. Jeff, Alan and Stan were there, though, supervising the placement of the flowers. Nick hoped none of the guests had hay fever—there were enough blooms here for an English country garden. But it was beautiful, and he wanted that for Jessica.

His cousin Carlo should be arriving soon. Nick couldn't wait to see him. He hadn't been able to make it to the rehearsal, but they'd spoken on the phone last night. As his best man, Carlo needed the rings, and also to go over the last-minute details. More than that, Nick wanted to talk. Carlo was the closest thing he had to an older brother, and he'd been married for more than three years.

"Nervous?"

Nick looked up from his seat in the front pew. Jeff was grinning at him, but Nick detected more behind the question than just polite ribbing. "Yes," he said. "It's bigger than I thought."

"You were here yesterday."

"But it wasn't real yesterday."

"Right," Jeff said, putting the arrangement of pink roses on the end of the pew. "It's all come together, though. I didn't think we could pull it off, but we did."

"Yes, and I thank you for that. You've done more than I could have ever hoped for." Nick leaned back, trying to get his chest to relax. "You really care about her, don't you?"

"Jess?" Jeff's grin grew wide. "She's my girl. I love her like a sister. Actually, I love her more than my sister, who, for the record, is a cold fish who wouldn't know a Berber carpet from a sheepdog.''

Nick smiled at the vivid description. "Have you two talked?"

"Me and my sister?"

"No, you and Jessica."

"About what?"

"This," Nick said, looking up at the dais.

"Sure."

Nick thought about how to ask his question, but no easy words came to him. Instead he just said, "Is she nervous, too?"

Jeff came over and sat down next to him. "Yeah, she's nervous. But I know she believes this is the best thing for the baby. She has no real family, you know. Her mother, what a case she is. She's not coming today, did you know that?"

"No, I didn't. Jessica didn't say."

"Mona has tickets to the ballet. Can you stand it? Some people don't deserve reproductive organs."

"Jessica will have a family now," Nick said, thinking of how much his mother and Theresa liked her.

"Yeah. Although I hate the idea of losing her to Rome."

"You think she'll come, then?"

"If she believes it's the best thing—"

"For the baby," Nick said, finishing for him.

"She's gonna be one hell of a mom."

Nick nodded. He remembered the list he'd read this morning. How Jessica was setting aside her own wishes for the good of the child. She'd clearly done a great deal of thinking, which didn't surprise him. Jessica was one of the most levelheaded people he'd ever met. But he also knew other things about her. She had difficulty believing in herself. Not in business, and not in friendship, but when it came to love, she was on unsteady ground. He'd discovered that their first night together. How frightened she was of taking risks. Of loving the wrong man. Of baring her soul.

Knowing this about her, he'd still gone on with his plans. Still talked her into this whirlwind wedding. So many things they hadn't discussed. How had he not known that her mother wasn't coming? Why hadn't Jessica confided in him, instead of Jeff?

"What's that about?"

"Hmm?"

Jeff shook his head. "That frown."

"I was thinking," Nick said. "For a man about to be married, I don't know my bride very well."

"Hey, you were the one with the stop watch ticking."

Nick nodded. He stood abruptly and turned to Jeff. "Would you excuse me, please?"

"Sure."

Nick walked down the aisle, picturing all his

friends and relatives who had dropped everything to fly to America. This room would soon be filled with people, but so few of them would be here for Jessica. Everything here was for his convenience, to suit his schedule.

Would telling Jessica he loved her wipe away all the selfish things he'd done in the last few weeks? Could he ever make it up to her?

"*Ciao,* Nicky!"

Nick looked up to see Carlo standing in the doorway. His cousin grinned at him as if they were still children. Nick felt better immediately. "Carlo, it's so good to see you!" Nick hurried toward the door and gave him a big hug. "I know it was difficult for you to get here."

"It's just that it isn't easy for Sophia when I'm gone. The children, you know?"

"I do," he said. "Come walk with me, cousin. I'd like to talk."

"Of course."

Nick led him to the street, and then he began from the beginning.

"IT'S ALMOST TIME."

Jessica smiled at Angelina, then took one last look in the mirror. This was it. Her wedding. She was about to become Mrs. Nick Carlucci. If only...

But she had promised herself there would be no second thoughts. She'd walked into this with her eyes open. Her child's future was secured, and it was up to her to make the most of the situation.

There was every chance that this marriage would turn out better than she could imagine. She knew Nick liked her and, in time, might come to love her. She clung to that thought as she went to pick up her bouquet.

The loud knock on the door startled her, and she looked from Angelina to Theresa, but they didn't seem to be expecting anyone, either. The small changing room was private, and the guests should have all been led in to the church.

The door opened, and Nick stepped inside.

Theresa gave a startled squeak, then tried to push him out again. "It's bad luck! You're not supposed to see her yet."

"I need to talk to her."

"It will have to wait. Now go!"

Nick stood his ground. "No, please. This must be done."

Jessica's heart thumped in her chest. This wasn't good. She knew it. Something terrible had happened that couldn't wait for the ceremony. Reluctantly, she moved her gaze to Nick's. He smiled at her, but there was a sadness in his eyes that made her throat close.

He walked over to her, took the bouquet and put it down on the table, then grasped both of her hands. His gaze caught hers and held it steady. "Do you love me?'' he asked, his voice so tender it made her more confused than ever. "Please, be honest. I need to know."

She knew it was no good lying to him. He could read her, he always had been able to do that. "Yes," she whispered.

"Do you believe I love you?"

She looked away. This was a much harder question. She knew he liked her, but love? She lifted her chin and met his gaze.

"I..."

"The truth, *carissima*. Please."

"No, I don't."

He nodded his head, as if she'd confirmed his own belief. "I do love you, Jessica. I didn't know it before, but I do now. Another thing I know is that my word isn't enough. I want you to believe, beyond any doubt or reason, that my love for you is real."

Jessica didn't know how to react. Was he telling her the truth? Or was this some crazy way of backing out of this hasty marriage? Why couldn't she see into his heart, the way he could see into hers? It wasn't fair.

"I've rushed you into this," he said. "And I apologize. I gave you no time to think things through. Or to really get to know me. I'd like to make up for that now, Jessica. If... When we get married, I want you to say yes because you want to. Not because you feel you have to, for the child. I need for you to see that I love you, *angelo mio.*"

Jessica tried to get her thoughts together. It had all happened so quickly, she wasn't at all sure how she should feel. She closed her eyes and took several deep breaths. She tried to feel something shift, a belief that he loved her click into place.

God, how she'd longed for those words! Yet she didn't believe them. She couldn't. The words weren't enough.

"I want to marry you," Nick said. "But I won't make this decision for you."

She looked at Theresa, at Angelina. They both appeared calm, but she knew they were thinking of the guests waiting outside, of the mess that would erupt if she told Nick she wanted to wait. Theresa's gaze went to her stomach, and Jessica realized she'd put a protective hand there.

"Don't worry," Nick said. "Whatever you decide, I'll do everything I can for the baby. He'll have a family, I give you my word."

This was what she'd wanted. Time. A chance to think things through. He was offering her the very thing she'd prayed for, yet it was almost unthinkable to say she wanted to call off the wedding.

"I'll wait, Jessica," he whispered. "For as long as it takes."

This was the single biggest decision she was ever going to make. It deserved time, and thought, and patience. Not just on her part, either. Nick had rushed into this whole thing, too. He deserved a chance to back out. Although she certainly hoped he wouldn't.

She nodded. It was all she had the strength for. If she tried to speak, she was going to cry, and she didn't want to do that. She'd done enough crying.

"I'll go make the announcement," Nick said. Then he leaned down and kissed her gently on the lips. "Next time," he whispered, "those tears will be from happiness. I give you my word."

Chapter Sixteen

Jessica stared at the slice of wedding cake on her plate. No one had wanted to eat it, after the wedding had been called off. So she'd frozen most of it. She hadn't eaten any, although sugary sweets were the only foods she really liked these days. Somehow, eating the cake seemed bad luck. It wasn't anything concrete, but she couldn't help feeling that if she kept it whole, the wedding would still take place, just as if nothing had happened.

Of course, that was nonsense. But she still couldn't do it. She put the plastic wrap back on the slice and slipped it into the freezer.

It didn't take a psychiatrist to understand why she'd tried to eat the cake today. Nick was at the airline. Getting his schedule. Making plans to leave her. In the two weeks since their canceled wedding, they'd spent a lot of time together, and while she felt she knew him better, there were still doubts.

Mostly about his long trips. He'd told her not to

worry. That he would be faithful. That he loved her. And mostly, she believed him. Mostly.

But when she was alone, she got scared. He'd tried to convince her to move to Rome, but she couldn't. Not for good, at least. She didn't want to leave her job or her friends now. Not while she was so uncertain of her future.

Time and again she thought she should just say yes. Marry him. Just believe in him. But it was no good. She just couldn't shake the image of Nick in his pilot's uniform. Of the women he'd meet. And she kept thinking of Angelina's words. It wasn't enough for Nick just to come back to her. She didn't want him to leave in the first place.

She wished Angelina and Theresa could have stayed longer. They had been so understanding, and so giving. They'd told her time and again that no matter what, she was family. The baby was family. It didn't matter if she married Nick, although they hoped she would.

Everyone had been wonderful about the wedding being called off. No one had cried foul, although she'd done a lot of explaining to Jeff and the others. In the end, they'd given her their total support. They'd let her know that if she decided not to marry, she'd have them to count on. Like a family.

The irony was not lost on her. All her life, the one thing she'd wanted was to belong. To have a family who loved her. Now that she'd called off her wedding, her dream had come .rue. She had what she'd longed for.

She also realized that a large parc of her decision to marry Nick in the first place was because of that dream. She'd said yes so she could belong. But the marriage was no longer needed. Not for that. Marrying Nick was now about one thing only—their love for each other.

She looked down at her yellow pad. The question on top was one she didn't know how to answer. Yesterday, the response would have been a resounding yes, but today she wasn't nearly as sure. Did she love Nick? Did she love him for the right reasons? Or did she only love him for the things he could give her?

Now that she knew she didn't have to face the future alone, was marriage something she wanted? What would it really be like, with him gone so much? Did she honestly believe he loved her enough to be faithful?

It all came down to trust, which was something she wasn't very familiar with. The one truth she'd believed since childhood was the fact that people were untrustworthy. That love was dangerous. That the only person she could count on was herself. Yet, that wasn't true anymore, was it?

She could count on Jeff. On Stan, and Paul and Alan. They had come through for her, many times.

Right this minute, Jeff and Stan were at the new house, designing the nursery.

She could count on Angelina and Theresa. They'd proved themselves to be kind and generous in every way.

And she could count on Nick…for certain things, at least. He'd be there financially for her and the baby. He'd be there emotionally, for the baby. But could she count on him to be there for her? To love her in sickness and in health? For the rest of their lives?

Maybe that was a question no one could answer, but surely when other people got married they didn't have this kind of doubt. But then, most people who got married knew each other far better than she knew Nick.

What were his favorite colors? How did he learn to fly? Was he allergic to anything? What did he want out of life? Of course, he didn't know any of those things about her, either. Was marriage the time to discover the answers, or were the answers the clues to whether she should marry?

One thing was clear. She'd never been more confused in her life. The problem was how to fix that. She sighed. How had life gotten so complicated? Looking up at the clock, she saw she had to shower. Nick would be back from the airport soon. They were going to the beach. What would happen after that? She had no idea.

NICK PRESSED ON THE GAS, grateful to be moving again, even if it was just a few feet. There had been an accident on the 405, and he'd been stuck in traffic for the last hour, watching the planes take off and land from Los Angeles International. He'd done some thinking, watching those planes. Going back to work was something he wanted, right? Then why did he feel so badly?

He knew it bothered Jessica that she'd be alone a great deal of the time, but what occurred to him while he was in the Alitalia office was that *he'd* be without *her*. That hadn't been a problem before. Now, it was. He wanted to be with her. All the time. He wanted to be there for the pregnancy. The birth. And surely he wanted to be there after the baby came. He didn't see how he could do both.

Unless, of course, he changed jobs. If he made his home base Los Angeles, and went on local flights only. That hadn't appealed to him before, but now? It would still mean he would be away from home, but not that often. Certainly nothing like the time he'd be away on international flights.

He sat with that decision as he inched his way on the freeway. She'd be pleased, he thought, with this plan. At least he hoped so. For the first time since he'd met Jessica, he couldn't read her. The last few weeks, she'd been moody and a little distant. Angelina had told him not to worry. He'd given Jessica a great deal to think about. And she'd suggested he do some thinking, too.

Not just about his job, but about his future. About his commitment to this new life he wanted so badly.

If he married Jessica, it was for the rest of his life. Could he do that? He wasn't sure. But he did know that the thought of living the rest of his life without her was untenable.

He remembered the day she'd arrived at his villa. That awful day when he'd hurt her, and Gina and Libby, so badly. That had been the turning point for him. When he'd seen Jessica's feet. When he saw she'd climbed the trellis. He'd fallen in love with her then, although he hadn't realized it. That was why he hadn't been able to write to her. Why he'd had to take time off and fly halfway around the world.

There had to be a way to convince her that marrying him was the right thing to do. But he had to be careful. No more pushing, no more making decisions for the both of them without talking to her first.

The problem was that Jessica was such a logical creature. She would have to be sure. All those cons on her yellow pad would have to turn to pros. A daunting task. He barely knew how to begin.

It had always been easy with women before. Not because he was so special, but because he didn't care. Not really. It was all temporary. He'd never let himself feel strongly about any one woman. And he'd made sure that no woman cared about him. Always, he'd told them that he was not serious.

Someone honked, and he realized that traffic had begun to move. He drove quickly now, past the wreck on the side of the road, to his exit. But he didn't stop thinking.

THE BEACH WAS ALMOST empty. A man walked with his dog, a woman read under an umbrella. Several surfers bobbed in the waves. Nick took Jessica's hand in his and led her down the steps to the sand.

She remembered the last time she'd been to the beach with him. They'd walked and walked, and she'd told him more in those hours than she'd admitted to any of her friends in years. He'd prompted her, eased her into the conversation, and somehow she'd felt safe. He'd known exactly what questions to ask, and she hadn't hesitated to answer him truthfully.

He smiled at her as he spread the blanket a few feet from the shoreline. "Good?"

She nodded, then sat down to take off her shoes. He joined her, slipping off his Italian loafers and his socks, then rolling up his pant legs, just like he'd done all those months ago. She let her gaze move over him and felt that strange tightness in her stomach that only he could produce. His blue polo shirt hugged his muscular back, and his biceps bunched and relaxed as he fixed his pant legs. When he stood up, he blocked the sun with his body, and the outline of him with his broad chest and slim, tight hips made her want much more than a walk on the beach.

Whatever their problems, they weren't about sex. She'd never been more excited by a man. Never felt this physical pull that made her inarticulate and almost feral in her desire. He hadn't just known how to talk to her. He'd known how to make love to her. She'd never had to say a word. He just knew. Even the first time, he'd known just where to touch, how hard, how soft, how long. It was as if she'd never made love before.

"Are you all right?"

She smiled and held out her hands. He took them and pulled her up, right into his arms. She couldn't help herself. She kissed him, and when her lips touched his, she felt herself relax completely. God, how she loved being this close. Touching him, tasting him. He filled the empty spaces inside her.

He broke the kiss gently, then smiled. "Are you sure you want to do this? We could go back to your apartment."

She grinned. "No, we'll walk. Then we'll go back to my apartment."

"Perhaps we'll jog, yes?"

Her laughter felt good, and she realized she

hadn't laughed in too long. Nick could always make her laugh, at least when she wasn't neck deep in an ocean of doubt. The only time she felt completely at ease was when they were like this. When their bodies took over.

She stepped back and took his hand, leading him to the shore. When she got to the wet sand, she curled her toes, loving the feel of it. A wave came up and the white bubbles washed over her feet. Cold as only the Pacific in summer can be. She sighed, content for the first time in days.

They began walking, and for a long while, they didn't speak. Jessica stared out over the ocean at the surfers and beyond them to the few boats on the horizon. Then she looked back at Nick, and that view was better still.

He was so beautiful. She hoped the baby would take after him. Girl or boy. She wanted her child to have his thick dark hair, his deep brown eyes and mostly that incredible profile.

"May I ask you a question?" Nick said.

"Yes, of course."

"Why didn't you tell me about your mother?"

Her throat tightened for just a second, then she relaxed again. "I'm not sure," she said. "I didn't want to spoil things, I guess."

"You think I wouldn't have understood?"

"Well, Mona isn't like Angelina. Not even close."

He looked at her for a long while. "Did I ever tell you about my father?"

She shook her head.

He took a deep breath, then squeezed her hand tight for a moment. "My father was a very good businessman. He traded in the stock market, bought and sold companies. He was ahead of his time in that way. A true entrepreneur. He made us very wealthy. I don't think we've ever talked about that, have we?"

"Well, I know you have money. The house, the villa."

"I have a great deal of money, Jessica. It's mostly in investments, but I also own a lot of property all over Europe. Our child will never have to worry about money. Ever. And neither will you."

"Your father?"

"Ah, yes. He was a very smart man. But he could be cruel. He didn't treat my mother very well."

"She told me she loved him very much."

"She did. And I believe he loved her, too. But that didn't stop him from hurting her. He never even tried to hide his mistresses. In fact, he was proud of the other women."

Nick walked quietly for a moment, staring at the water. "He told me that marriage was for women, not men. That you got married to have children, and that was a good thing. But real men couldn't be satisfied with one woman for a whole lifetime.''

"Oh, Nick."

"How much he hurt Mama. She cried and cried, all because she loved him so much. By the time I was a young man, she'd stopped crying. She'd made peace with the situation. But I didn't. Even though I loved my father, I hated him, too."

"I'm sorry."

"So you see, *carissima,* I understand. I see that you want so much for the baby. That you want to give our child what you didn't have."

"And you," she said. "You didn't want to be like your father."

"No. I didn't. I don't."

"But you're frightened?"

"I think yes. But now that I see, I don't think it's too much of a danger."

They fell into silence once more as they continued walking. Seabirds found tiny morsels to eat all around them. Jessica let go of Nick's hand and slipped her arm around his waist. He moved so he could hold her shoulder, while she rested her head against his. So much to think about. She understood more now. But she still didn't have a complete picture of Nick. That would take a very long time. It occurred to her that it would be time very well spent.

"Nick?"

"Yes?"

"Why me?"

"What do you mean?"

"Why do you want to marry me?"

Nick stopped and gave her a funny little smile. "I was hoping you'd ask," he said. Then he reached into his back pocket and brought out a small notepad. Like a boy handing his teacher a shiny apple, he gave it to her.

She looked down and smiled. There, in very small, neat print, was a list. The title was Why I Should Marry Jessica. Underneath that was only one sentence. But it was a good one. *Because I love her.*

"Turn the page, Cara."

She did. It was empty.

"You see?" he said, touching her face with the back of his hand. "No cons. Only pros."

"Nick, it's still awfully fast."

"So we take our time. We marry when it's right for you. No rushing."

"But with your schedule…"

"About that," he said. "I wanted to discuss it with you first, of course, but I was thinking…"

"Yes?"

"I was thinking of applying for a new job. Here in Los Angeles. With a local airline."

Her heart thumped so hard in her chest that she

could barely hear the ocean. "But you don't want to fly local runs."

"I didn't, that's true. Things change."

"I don't want you to do this for me, Nick. You'll be unhappy, and that won't work. You'll just end up resenting me."

"You're right. If I was just doing it for you, I would be unhappy. But I'm not, Jessica. I'm doing it for me. I don't want to be away from you." His hand moved to her stomach, where he rubbed her gently. "I want to watch the baby grow, from now until he goes to college."

"Are you sure?" she asked, hardly believing this could be real. "Are you very sure?"

He nodded. "Even if we weren't going to have a baby, I'd still want the same thing. I love you, *angelo mio*. With all my heart." He leaned forward and kissed her. Softly, tenderly.

Then he broke the kiss but stayed so close she felt the warmth of his breath linger on her lips. "Will you marry me, Jessica? Be my wife?"

Jessica felt the cool sand under her feet. The sun on her shoulders. The wind teasing her hair. She'd remember this moment for the rest of her life. Every sensation. Every detail. But most of all, she'd remember the look in Nick's eyes, and how she knew without doubt, without pause, that this was the man she would love forever. And that he loved her right back.

Then, she remembered another moment—a coin tossed in the water, a wish. It hadn't come true. She *was* a fool for love. A crazy, contented, blissful fool, who'd never stopped loving Nick. For once in her life, she was glad wishes don't always come true.

"Yes, my Nicolo," she whispered. "I will marry you. I'll be your wife."

Epilogue

Three months later

Dear Libby and Gina,

I'm just delighted with the idea of this round-robin letter. So much has happened to all of us since that afternoon in Rome!

Gina, Jackson sounds like a dream. I'm so happy for you! But you didn't give me near enough details about your wedding. What did you wear? Were there a lot of dignitaries there? And I'm dying to know where you took your honeymoon!

I think I'll be seeing you in Italy, but more on that in a moment.

Libby! You sound so happy! Your Ethan also sounds just wonderful. And the two little ones sound simply adorable. I can't wait to meet them all at your wedding.

Can you believe it? Both of you married.

Well, guess what, girls. Me, too!

Hold on to yourselves, 'cause you're going to faint. I married *Nick*.

Are you finished screaming yet? Okay, so let me explain. See, it turned out that when we all met in Nick's bedroom, I was pregnant. Only I didn't find out about it till the next day. Then I went home, but guess who showed up a few days later? That's right. The louse. Only it turned out that he wasn't quite the louse we'd imagined.

You see, he really didn't mean to hurt any of us, and he still feels awful about what happened. And of course, he wanted to do the honorable thing and marry me. The funny part is, we sort of fell in love. Hard. Wonderfully. Happily. Forever.

Okay, okay. I'll stop. But not until I tell you that I've never been more content in my life.

The wedding itself? That's a whole other story, but guess where we ended up having the ceremony? At the Trevi Fountain! Yes, right where we threw our coins and made our wishes! Can you stand it? It was so perfect. His whole family was there, and, oh, did you know the woman in the negligee was his sister? My sister, now.

Nick and I are back in the States, but we're going to spend several months each year in Rome. That's what I was talking about, Gina. Maybe we can get together when I'm there? From your letter, I think you won't have transferred back to New York yet. We'd both love to see you, and to meet Jackson. Libby? Maybe you could make plans to join us, too? I'd love to have a reunion. And if you bring Ethan and the kids, that will be all the better.

Anyway, while I was at the fountain, I threw in another coin for each one of us. The old legend turned out to be true...sort of. I mean, no matter what we wished, each one of us got our heart's desire, right? Not just one. So I figured, why not? Why not make three more wishes? Only this time, it truly was for all three of us to come back to Rome. I'll bet they still have our table waiting at the bistro.

Well, my friends, Nick is home, and I must go. Did I tell you he's not flying internationally any longer? Nope, our Nick is now based in Los Angeles, flying to and from San Francisco. He's home pretty much every night. Which is a good thing. I'd miss him too much if he stayed away longer.

Write back soon, and tell me how you are.

I want all the news! I miss you guys.

Love,
Jessica

P.S.—Nick sends you both big kisses! From our hearts to yours, *ciao!*

The Gifts of Christmas

**Join three of your favorite historical romance
authors as they celebrate the festive season
in their own special style!**

Mary Balogh
Merline Lovelace &
Suzanne Barclay

**bring you a captivating collection
of historical romances.**

Indulge in the seasonal delights of Regency and
medieval England and share in the discovery of
unforgettable love with *The Gifts of Christmas.*

Available in November 1998,
at your favorite retail store.

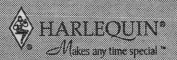

HARLEQUIN®
Makes any time special ™

LOOK FOR OUR FOUR FABULOUS MEN!

Each month some of today's bestselling authors bring
four new fabulous men to Harlequin American Romance.
Whether they're rebel ranchers, millionaire power brokers
or sexy single dads, they're all gallant princes—and
they're all ready to sweep you into lighthearted fantasies
and contemporary fairy tales where anything is possible
and where all your dreams come true!

You don't even have to make a wish…
Harlequin American Romance will grant your every desire!

Look for Harlequin American Romance
wherever Harlequin books are sold!

Christmas Is For Kids

This Christmas, some of your favorite
Harlequin American Romance authors bring
you brand-new stories that will warm your heart!
In December 1998, don't miss:

#753 SMOOCHIN' SANTA
by Jule McBride

#754 BABY'S FIRST CHRISTMAS
by Cathy Gillen Thacker

#755 COWBOY SANTA
by Judy Christenberry

#756 GIFT-WRAPPED DAD
by Muriel Jensen

Available at your favorite retail outlet.

HARLEQUIN®
Makes any time special ™

HARLEQUIN®

A M E R I C A N ❖ R O M A N C E®
®

COMING NEXT MONTH
Christmas Is For Kids

#753 SMOOCHIN' SANTA by Jule McBride
The Little Matchmaker
Little Christy Holt was the wiliest seven-year-old to hit Mistletoe
Mountain in years. Within minutes of having pregnant cabbie
Nikki Ryder drive her to Jon Sleet's mountain retreat, she'd created a
crazy story that Jon was her father…and just by looking at her,
Nikki could tell that the child wanted to create a ready-made family
by Christmas.

#754 BABY'S FIRST CHRISTMAS by Cathy Gillen Thacker
The ordinarily calm ER doctor Michael Sloane broke a sweat when he
met Kate Montgomery…and saw her belly full of his baby. He'd never
expected the frisson of longing to be a father that zinged through his
heart, nor the instant attraction to the very pregnant Kate. Darned if
he didn't want to be a daddy and a husband to her by Christmas.

#755 COWBOY SANTA by Judy Christenberry
When cowboy Sam Crawford played Santa for the kids of
Saddle, Wyoming, he thought it his duty to be sure the kids got their
wishes. Most especially when the son of that knockout newcomer
Joni Evans asked Santa for a horse, a train…and a daddy!

#756 GIFT-WRAPPED DAD by Muriel Jensen
Janie Cummings and her baby brother knew the moment Joe Carpenter
walked into their mother's bed-and-breakfast that he was Santa's "gift"
to them. Now if they could just convince their mother, Maribeth, that
she needed him….

AVAILABLE THIS MONTH:

Look us up on-line at: http://www.romance.net